SO-ABA-785

A woman's perfume wafted over him

Carl Lyons knew it was Tabina who stood at the side of his hospital bed. She moved closer, and suddenly Lyons felt cold fingers rest against his throat.

Tabina's fingers found a nerve behind his clavicle. She squeezed, sending a crippling numbness through Lyon's body.

The female terrorist exerted more pressure. "On your feet, *now.*"

Lyons refused to move. Consciousness was slipping.

"If I apply any more pressure, he'll pass out," warned Tabina, turning to the man who waited by the door. "Find an orderly and a gurney," she ordered as she tried once again to get Lyons to his feet. "We'll have to do this the hard way."

The pressure became intense, and darkness quickly enveloped Carl Lyons.

*

"Able Team will go anywhere, do anything, in order to complete their mission."
—*West Coast Review of Books*

Mack Bolan's

ABLE TEAM

#1 Tower of Terror
#2 The Hostaged Island
#3 Texas Showdown
#4 Amazon Slaughter
#5 Cairo Countdown
#6 Warlord of Azatlan
#7 Justice by Fire
#8 Army of Devils
#9 Kill School
#10 Royal Flush
#11 Five Rings of Fire
#12 Deathbites
#13 Scorched Earth
#14 Into the Maze
#15 They Came to Kill
#16 Rain of Doom
#17 Fire and Maneuver
#18 Tech War
#19 Ironman

#20 Shot to Hell
#21 Death Strike
#22 The World War III Game
#23 Fall Back and Kill
#24 Blood Gambit
#25 Hard Kill
#26 The Iron God
#27 Cajun Angel
#28 Miami Crush
#29 Death Ride
#30 Hit and Run
#31 Ghost Train
#32 Firecross
#33 Cowboy's Revenge
#34 Clear Shot
#35 Strike Force
#36 Final Run
#37 Red Menace
#38 Cold Steel
#39 Death Code

ABLE TEAM.
Death Code

Dick Stivers

A GOLD EAGLE BOOK FROM
WORLDWIDE.

TORONTO • NEW YORK • LONDON • PARIS
AMSTERDAM • STOCKHOLM • HAMBURG
ATHENS • MILAN • TOKYO • SYDNEY

First edition December 1988

ISBN 0-373-61239-7

Special thanks and acknowledgment to
Larry Lind for his contribution to this work.

The scorching African sun flooded the Koran-scrolled windows, casting shadows of the scriptures across the long conference table. Ignoring the divine writ, fifteen robed commanders hid their impatience.

Surrounded by luxury and constantly entertained, the Brotherhood's staff officers clearly enjoyed their pampered status. They looked forward to completing the last item on the agenda. Comrade Major Omar Khalid had promised to introduce them to a group of blond European prostitutes when their business was settled.

Everyone watched Comrade General Farid Mousa as the secretary read the last request. Their leader rolled a pen back and forth under his palm. Finally he nodded to the Russian adviser.

"It's a waste," spat the general. "How could an officer so dedicated to the Brotherhood seek such personal glory?" Mousa surveyed the staff officers' eyes for agreement. Nodding, each man returned his look, then lowered his gaze to the table.

"He sees himself as a modern Muhammad," offered Comrade Major Khalid. "His financial gains from oil have made him believe he's qualified to lead the Muslim world against the Western imperialists."

The general slammed his fist on the table so hard that the pen hopped. "Then let Allah's Blade finance their own jihad. Comrade Khalid, write the rejection letter, and I'll sign it. The rest of you are dismissed."

The Russian adviser remained behind. Cleaning his nails with a small pocketknife, Colonel Markus Konstantin watched the Arabs retreat to their waiting entertainment. Contempt should have drawn a curse from his lips, but he exercised the patience he'd learned while working in Arab embassies for the past thirteen years. The oil-rich playboys lacked the dedication of the KGB agents he'd worked with during his career.

Removing nonexistent grit from already clean fingernails was a habit he'd picked up during long stakeouts with his mentor, General Igor Botechev. "Keeps me constantly aware of the good Russian earth I used to work in with these soft white hands," he said if anyone dared to question his actions. "Don't forget the basics. Our hands belong to the Party and to Mother Russia. Someday comrades with hands like ours will rule the entire world."

The squeak of a chair brought Konstantin out of his reverie. Without moving his head, he glanced at General Mousa. Unaware that the colonel's eyes were not occupied with fingernail inspection, the general allowed his inner feelings to mold his face. Hatred covered every suntanned inch.

"Your staff seemed a bit preoccupied today, General Mousa."

"Don't be fooled by the relaxed lion. He will strike when necessary, but he plays as well as he fights." Secretly Farid Mousa acknowledged the truth of the accusation, but he would never publicly agree with the man or with any Russian. He despised them for their never-ending exploitation of his people. He revealed his agitation by tapping the palm of his hand with his pen.

Someday, he thought, masking his feelings while he imagined dragging the Russian behind his stallion, you'll feel Berber justice.

Konstantin continued to work on his nails. "Tell me about this rebel you refuse to support."

"Colonel Razul? He was one of our most dedicated warriors."

"What happened?"

"A professional rebel with a vision as magnificent as the great desert, but a soul as small as one handful of sand."

"Translate."

The general smoothed his mustache with the shaft of his pen. "He's so full of himself that there's no room for dedication to Lenin's vision, let alone anyone else's."

"A loner?"

Mousa pursed his lips. "No, more of a reject. He keeps getting into trouble because he refuses to obey his superiors. In his mind no one is smart enough to command him."

"And his military skills?"

"Excellent, up to a point. He performs very well, but his tactical and administrative skills will never exceed those of a lieutenant."

Colonel Konstantin folded his pocketknife. "Disobedient soldiers, no matter how skilled, are useless. Let's have dinner, my friend, and discuss our next operation."

2

The immaculately dressed commander of Allah's Blade felt the icy hand of Arab politics exert its pressure once again. He reread the hand-delivered communiqué.

Dear Comrade Colonel Razul:
The Revolutionary Council has studied your request for support of Allah's Blade. While we commend your zeal, we feel splinter groups weaken the cause. With regret, we deny your request and encourage you to return to the true jihad.
We will purge the world of Western oppression with or without your help. Your personal skills are great. The Brotherhood needs you. It is a waste of your gifts to remain idle. Reconsider. Join the cause.

Comrade General Farid Mousa, for the Brotherhood's Revolutionary Council.

Short even for an Arab, Colonel Ziyad Razul stretched to his full four-foot-six height. His stubby fingers crushed his group's death notice. Whistling through his teeth, he screamed at the messenger, "Out of my sight. Tell your leader that Allah's Blade will carve a victory so great the Brotherhood will beg to unite with us."

The courier, having been warned of Razul's possible reaction, saluted calmly. "Am I to take that as a negative response, comrade colonel, sir?"

Shocked by the young man's insolence, Razul moved within inches of the boy. "Son, when you regain consciousness, you may tell those idiots that Allah's Blade totally rejects the Brotherhood. In fact, I seriously doubt their loyalty."

The messenger had also been warned not to let Razul touch him, but he couldn't gracefully squirm out from under the colonel's hand. Steel-hard fingers jabbed into a spot just below the upper edge of his trapezius. Pain coursed through the boy's body, and he folded to the carpet before he could free himself from the colonel's fingers.

Whistling, the rejected commander recovered his swagger stick. He pointed it at the unconscious messenger, started to speak, shook his head and strode out. Now the future of Allah's Blade rested totally with Razul, not with the dogs who had deserted him.

ALONZO BLACK'S THIN FRAME vibrated like a tuning fork. The blonde turned the corner toward him. He sucked the morning air through his lips, picturing her body close to his. She moved closer. She was wearing a thin blue tank top, and the nipples of her bouncing breasts testified to the chilly morning. His breathing shortened. This was living, he thought.

The son of an Italian immigrant worker who had saved and wisely invested his meager earnings, Alonzo Black had never worked a day in his life. Bright enough to go to college, he had milked his father for permanent student status. He was on his fourth university and had only one goal: to be rich enough to attract unlimited numbers of women—without working at it. Alonzo cherished the belief that one only needed money to surround oneself with feminine beauty.

A voyeur for most of his life, Alonzo never passed the point of looking and then offering what he considered his 'sweet invitations.' His gross comments always drove even the most available women away. Only prostitutes had experienced his amateurish fumblings.

The blonde was backlit by the slanting rays of the morning sun. Her hair resembled a bronze bonfire. Ten feet separated them.

Alonzo's armpits dampened. His mind leapfrogged common sense. "I'm in love with your sweet ass" slipped through passion-stiffened lips.

"Excuse me?" asked the girl, unaware of what he'd mumbled. "Were you speaking to me?"

"Sure was, sweet-ass mama. Let's you and me find out what really turns you on."

Offended by his blatant offer, she glanced in each direction, looking for the quickest escape route.

As usual, Alonzo read anything less than an immediate counterattack as a positive reaction. He leaned toward her. "Like the idea, huh? I don't blame you. I've got a room over—"

She had to stand on tiptoe, but she managed a right-handed slap that knocked the graduate student's head back. "Why don't you take your own sweet ass and get the hell out of here?" She stormed away without a backward glance.

The Ph.D. candidate from the La Jolla Institute for Advanced Oceanographic Studies had finally found himself beached. He had been thrown out of the school for unacceptable conduct. Known as "Alonzo the Lech" to his classmates, the part-time teaching assistant had been caught offering to swap high grades for sexual favors.

Alonzo Black was a microbiologist; the title of his doctoral thesis was to have been "The Application of Mutated Oil-consuming Bacteria as a Weapon." He'd been funded by an unnamed oil company that was furious about his dismissal, but the school had promised it could easily duplicate his efforts and accelerate the program. The company had bought it.

Back in his apartment, Alonzo shuffled and reshuffled the cards. He hadn't won a game of solitaire for three hands. Time to cheat. Slowly he placed the cards on his bed, seven across. Seven—they'll be paying me more than seven million, he thought. He stopped to admire a *Playboy* centerfold for the umpteenth time.

"I'll soon be able to buy as many of you lovelies as I want," he said, his eyes caressing the pages. With a sigh, the thirty-six-year-old student heaved his six-foot-four-inch, one-hundred-seventy-pound frame from the bed. He couldn't move around, because his apartment was ankle-deep in trash. Pizza boxes, paper bags filled with Styrofoam McDonald's hamburger containers, empty cups and three weeks' worth of dirty clothes littered the room.

Alonzo Black didn't know the meaning of the word *patience*. But he had to be patient now. Everything was on hold until he could make his deal through his former student, Ibrahim Mohammet. Then...party time. Alonzo did a barefoot Irish jig that sent trash flying, singing "G-String Boogie" in a cracked falsetto.

"Ibrahim, my friend," he chortled, "in two weeks I'm going to step out of this delightful abode and into the arms of any woman I desire." He kicked a pile of dirty shirts into the air and reached for his copy of *Playboy*.

THE HEAT of the North African afternoon was stifling inside the small, spartan room. But Colonel Ziyad Razul, a true son of the desert, ignored it. His uniform wasn't even damp. A friend of heat, Razul relaxed, but the sweating boy in front of him squirmed.

Miracles didn't just walk into a Libyan terrorist camp asking to be used. But the more Ziyad listened, the more excited he became. If this frightened idiot spoke the truth, Allah's Blade might now hold the bargaining chip it needed to recruit more men.

He turned toward his heavily perspiring lieutenant.

"By all that is holy, how can you believe this—this con man?" Ziyad swatted the unpainted table with his swagger stick.

"But, sir, he's your nephew. Besides, everything he's told us checked out before we called you. We've found no holes in his story." Lieutenant Akmet's fright showed. His superior was beginning to whistle, and whenever Colonel Razul whistled, something terrible happened to somebody.

Ziyad turned back to his nephew.

"Now, Mr. Mohammet." The colonel spoke in insulting English instead of Arabic. "Why do you come to us with this preposterous story? Only traitors try to exploit and extort money from their own people. You must have lost your heart for our cause while studying in those infidel schools in America."

A low whistle chilled the perspiring Lieutenant Akmet.

A weak and peaceful scholar, Ibrahim recognized trouble when he saw it, and he saw it now. It glowered at him. Instead of being welcomed as a hero, he'd received the sort of abuse usually reserved for a turncoat. He couldn't recall Libya's heat ever having been so stifling before. His uncle's eyes glistened, and his shoulders hunched forward like a cobra's hood. His burning eyes hypnotized the boy.

"But Uncle Ziyad," Ibrahim sobbed. It was so different from what he'd expected. He remembered his last binge with Alonzo. They'd celebrated the idea of selling the new strain of the oil-eating bacteria. It had seemed so simple. Just let the rich crazies know that instant glory was attainable. After all, they should have a right to sell their idea to whoever demonstrated interest. A few million wouldn't hurt any of the oil sheikhs. How could something so simple end up so terrifying?

Razul jerked Ibrahim out of his reverie by gathering the front of his shirt in one strong hand.

3

One o'clock in the afternoon. Summer. A southern California beach, and a sense of peace for the first time in one hell of a long spell. A cotton-thick cloud drifted away from the sun, and warm rays heated his muscular legs. Carl Lyons's mind drifted between memories of teenage surfing and an endless blur of remembered battles. Each wave breaking over the rocks in La Jolla Cove was like a miniature burst of gunfire.

"...seven, eight, nine. I got nine on this side. I'll have to wait until he turns over."

There was the sound of another female voice counting: "five, six.... Look at that beauty on his left pec!"

With the word *pec*, a switch snapped in Carl Lyons's mind. He opened one eye. Two bikini-clad beauties were concentrating on his motionless body with all the interest of unemployed morticians.

The one who liked his left pec giggled. "Let's tickle him to see if he'll roll over."

Carl decided to see if these southern California lovelies could count past nine. He turned onto his stomach.

"See, see, I told you some of them were bullet holes that went all of the way through," chirped the one in the blue bikini.

"I'll bet he's a hit man," said the other.

"Couldn't be a smart one with all of those scars," answered her friend.

That did it.

The Able Team warrior rolled over again and sat up. "You're ruining my nap with your counting. Can I help?"

Startled by Lyons's offer, both girls retreated; then, spotting the sparkle in the rugged blonde's eyes, they attacked.

"We had a bet on you," blue bikini said when she finally managed to speak.

"Do I look like a horse?" Lyons complained.

The red bikini's owner, a voluptuous, blue-eyed, auburn-haired giggler, ran her gaze over his body. "In some ways—"

Her embarrassed friend pulled the ends of her dark brown hair over her face. "Virginia, you are too much!"

With a sigh, Lyons stood, brushing sand from his muscular thighs. "If you're not going to tell me what the bet is, I'll be moving on."

"I'll tell," blurted Virginia, grabbing his hand. "It was scars."

"Scars?"

"I bet Sherry that you had more on your back than on the front."

Lyons looked from one to the other. "And?"

"Sherry won. She figured a brute of a man like you would take his troubles head-on."

Lyons chuckled. "Pretty close."

"How did you get them?" asked Virginia.

"Termites," said the Able Team warrior; he was warming up to both of them.

"Sure, sure," laughed Sherry. "Termites that go *bang bang*."

"What does the winner of this bet get for her prize?"

Both girls grinned. They looked at each other, each waiting for the other to speak.

Virginia finally raised her chin. "The winner, Sherry, gets—you."

"How do you know I'm available?" He asked the question with apparent detachment, but he caught himself flexing his lats.

"No rings, no date, no kids," answered Virginia.

"No problems." Lyons smiled.

Sherry walked over and slipped her arm around his and tugged. "I'm the winner. Where are you taking me for lunch? Bye, Virginia. Somebody had to lose."

"Well, winner, where to?" shrugged Lyons.

"I've wanted to visit that cave under the store up on Cave Street. They tell me it's spooky and a little bit...romantic. But first let's take a quick look at that old house over there." Hand in hand, they started across the street.

As they neared the sidewalk, a baritone voice yelled, "Hey, hey, mama. You got a great ass. Bring it over here for a real man! Dump that delicate little pinkie tourist. C'mon over here, where the men are."

Another offered, "We be da best, baby, da best."

Able Team's Ironman turned toward the voices. It was more than the insults; something was forcing old memories to the surface. He knew the first voice. "Wait for me by the steps," he told Sherry.

"No. You don't have to defend my honor."

"Go."

The look in his eyes told Sherry not to pursue the argument.

Lyons covered the ground between himself and the smartass in five long strides. Seated behind the steering wheel of a black Cadillac, a big Oriental dressed in leather pants and vest grinned at him. A vivid scar ran from his left temple to his chin. Three more punks made it a full load.

"You got a problem?" asked Lyons, leaning on the roof.

The Able Team warrior's memory clicked as he stared down at the punk. The leering face took Lyons back to his LAPD days. He shuddered, and a frightening memory broke loose. The smell of cordite...

A bone-rattling explosion had slammed its fist into Ironman's chest. Carl Lyons had come within two feet of being decapitated by a booby trap. He had landed on his back, sprawled across a curb. A maniacal laugh had tucked itself under the gray blur of his consciousness as he'd fought to remain alert.

Genghis, watching from the safety of a doorway, swaggered out, waiting for the cop's head to clear.

Unable to move, Ironman lay helpless, faintly aware of the approaching steps.

"Hey, pig. Nap time is over. Open your eyes and say hello to your teacher."

Recognizing the voice, Lyons tried to respond, but words refused to pass his numb lips. His eyelids felt as heavy as forty-five-pound barbell plates. With typical Ironman tenacity, Lyons bench-pressed his eyes open. Genghis's ankles filled his horizon.

The gang leader spit on Lyons's badge. "Is the little pig going to join the party?"

"Waste him," came from a voice on the other side of the fallen officer's vision.

"Let's pull the legs off this fly while we have the chance," commanded the gang leader. "We have one of

L.A.'s finest spread out here for our entertainment. Don't chugalug this opportunity... sip it.''

"Hey, man, that bomb is going to have the heat here real quick," complained a voice from behind Lyons's head. Genghis's Horde didn't want to get busted because their leader wanted to play games with one useless pig.

Genghis delivered a vicious kick to Lyons's jaw. "Now, compared to that little firecracker, a good kick is only a sip. Right, Mr. Lyons?" He kicked him again. "This pig's mine. Stay away."

Fighting the blur, Ironman inventoried his body. Pleased to feel his arms flex, he waited for the Chinese hood's next move.

Cheers from Genghis's gang brought another kick toward Lyons's head. In one motion, the prone cop jerked his head back, pushed his body onto its side and grabbed the heel of his assailant's other foot. With a *kiai* that was probably heard in San Diego, Lyons jerked the hood's standing foot out from under him. In a split second, Genghis lay sprawled atop his worst enemy.

"Sip this asshole," gritted Lyons, reaching for Genghis's throat. Everything wasn't as clear as Lyons would have liked it, but with both hands on the punk's throat, who needed to see?

Genghis tried prying the Ironman's fingers loose. Within seconds he, too, had a vision problem.

The hood's body went into spasms. Before Lyons could shove the jerking body off, a wailing siren broke into his consciousness.

"Orders or not, we're splitting," C.C., knife man of the Horde, yelled. He pulled an oversize bowie and hammered Ironman on the head with the handle. "I ain't killing no cop in public."

Lyons slipped back into unconsciousness. He didn't feel the gang leader being dragged away.

"Carl? Carl, you okay?"

"My Python—did they get my piece?" The semiconscious officer felt around him for his weapon.

"No, Carl. It's right here," the cop assured his partner as he helped him to his feet. Three more squad cars roared up, sirens wailing. The neighborhood was boiling with blue uniforms.

The lieutenant led Lyons to his car. "What happened?"

The upshot of the encounter had been the formation of a unit to deal specifically with the increasing number of gangs terrorizing L.A. Carl Lyons had been chosen to head the LAPD strike force. And now, years and many battles later, he looked down at the enemy he had failed to put behind bars.

Genghis's face came into focus again. "Where did you get enough balls to leave your turf? The big boys in L.A. run you off?" Ironman taunted.

"Well, well, if it isn't *former* L.A. police officer Mr. Carl 'Airborne' Lyons." The big Chinese laughed. "Don't you feel a little naked out in public without that little .357 Colt Python you always carried? At least you could spit-shine your badge." He stabbed his index finger into the middle of Lyons's chest.

The gesture was a mistake.

Ironman exploded. He grabbed Genghis's wrist, put his other hand under his elbow and, pressing upward, arm-barred his head into the car's roof. As soon as he heard the dull *clunk*, Lyons gripped the Oriental's wrist and yanked until the side of the surprised driver's head slammed against the doorframe.

The rest of the Cad's doors opened. But before the hoods were out, Lyons grasped the limp hand hanging out of the window and applied an aikido wrist flex.

"Shit," Genghis bellowed.

"Call off the dogs," Lyons ordered.

"Back off, back off! He's breaking my fuckin' arm."

Everyone settled back into the car. A flash of blue gunmetal caught Lyons's eye. He tightened his hold again.

"Tell the guy in the back seat to sit on his hardware."

The edges of Genghis's red sweatband were wet. Pure hatred glistened in his slitted eyes. "Do what the man says, we have more important business."

"But Genghis," a slender black complained, "we can't take this shit from a pig."

"Do it, man!" the Oriental ordered through clenched jaws.

Lyons smiled at the furious hood. He nodded. "'Nuff?"

Genghis nodded.

Relaxing his grip, Ironman turned. "My date and I accept your apologies."

Eyes closed, the driver of the Cadillac rubbed his left wrist. A large red welt crossed the vertical scar on his cheek.

Shaking her head, an awed young lady watched the poised warrior return from combat.

"Why are you shaking your head?"

"I don't believe what I just witnessed."

"What?"

"I'm more impressed by how you handled those hoods than by any TV cop movie I've ever seen. We don't have heroes like you running around Santa Barbara."

"Just part of the job, ma'am," he laughed. "If you'll excuse me for a moment, I'd like to wash my hands."

"GADGETS, WE'RE ON VACATION. Enjoy the delights of this jewel of a beach," Rosario Blancanales said.

"Vacation? Do you call voluntarily turning yourself into a lubricated slug with second-degree burns over twenty-five percent of your body a vacation?" Able Team's electronics genius shot back.

Pol, Able Team's "people person," could barely find the energy to counter Gadgets Schwarz. "I don't call running from one electronics seminar to another and listening for hours to some boy genius a vacation."

"The batteries I'm here to recharge are real batteries—with electrons," Gadgets retorted. "Here, in my heart," he said, tapping his chest.

"I believe it, I believe it." Blancanales laughed. "You're loaded with lead in your ass and acid on your tongue." He threw a handful of sand at his retreating friend, then rolled over, his light side up, and fell asleep.

Schwarz brushed the sand off his notebook and ran to his rented gray Citation. The lecture on electromagnetic interference started in twenty minutes. He looked back at the Casa's sea wall and waved. "Next time."

ALONZO REJOICED. The male voice on the phone had said they'd meet him in half an hour in front of the rest rooms at La Jolla Cove. Ibrahim must have struck pay dirt. Alonzo was ecstatic. He had even combed some of the knots out of his blond beard and tied his hair into a ponytail.

He ran down Cave Street to a large flat area that looked like a green blanket covered with multicolored tourists. His heart pounded, but not from the run. It was the possibility of being an inch away from becoming instantly rich. He arrived early. Sitting on the grass between the steps and the rest rooms, he evaluated everyone. Even little old ladies were suspect.

He was fenced in by dozens of pairs of legs shiny with lotion. To his right four senior citizens reveled in a hot shuffleboard game, and five wet-suited divers passed him, bragging about the gold-colored Garibaldi they'd seen.

A heavy-breasted, black-haired young woman wearing faded designer jeans and a halter top approached, twirling a pair of mirrored sunglasses in her right hand. She smiled at him.

Momentarily Alonzo forgot why he was waiting outside a rest room in La Jolla, California. Never—never—had such a sensuous woman given him a second look. He couldn't take his eyes off her.

She smiled, continuing to look into his face.

Maybe she's going to the john, he thought. He turned his head to see if she had another reason for smiling.

With the grace of a leopard, she picked her way between the group of divers and two occupied picnic blankets.

"Mr. Alonzo Black?"

Her honeyed voice crippled the microbiologist's brain as he tried to accept the fact she was actually addressing him.

"That's me." He laughed nervously, extending his hand.

The woman ignored his gesture. "If you would like to join us in a discussion of your alleged discovery, walk ahead of me to that yellow Mercedes parked across the street."

Alonzo realized that it was not a request but an order.

When they arrived at the car, Colonel Razul stepped out and opened the back door. He couldn't wait another second to meet this traitor who possessed the solution to Allah's Blade's problems.

In the driver's seat of a black Cadillac parked behind Razul's car, a mean-looking Oriental wearing a red headband tapped his inch-long fingernails on the dash. The Horde's chief refused to give up control of anything, even the driving. Three other hoods glared from the car.

"Give Genghis the directions, Tabina," Razul ordered, looking from his daughter to the Cadillac. "I want to get to know our friend a little better."

They drove out Highway 5 to the North County high-tech area. Complex after complex of genetic engineering companies filled the area. Dedicated scientists working on everything from pregnancy detection tests to supersecret drugs for wealthy pharmaceutical companies had flocked to southern California.

The avant-garde buildings in the area excited Razul. Manicured landscapes, generously sprinkled with contemporary sculptures, were accented by parking lots filled with European luxury cars.

"Look at the wealth we are going to liberate, Tabina. The cost of these corporate toys would keep Allah's Blade financed for years."

She placed a hand on her father's shoulder. "Before too long we'll have a piece of it."

They turned down a side street leading to a modern multicolored two-story building. It had a cubist look, like a set of kids' blocks thrown into a heap at random.

Alternating pastel cubes with sides of glass gave an impression of money—lots of it.

A dramatic sculpture—a six-foot bronze Bunsen burner leaning against an Erlenmeyer flask—graced the lawn. It had the patina of great age and bore a sign that read *Dnathro*.

"This is it," Razul announced. "Our comrades in Carlsbad have loaned it to us for three weeks. The new owners will not occupy it for two months, and the guard is one of our people. Everything is in place."

"Wow! This is great, but what do we need it for?" Alonzo questioned. They were the first words he had uttered since getting into the car.

"This is home until you prove what Ibrahim said is true."

"Won't take long." The tall prisoner laughed. "Just as long as it takes you to count out the money." He stroked his beard and wiggled his eyebrows.

"First we need proof. Then we discuss your fee."

THE DISCUSSION had degenerated into an argument. Carl Lyons stood at the pay phone overlooking La Jolla Cove. "I'm sure of it," he said. "I saw Colonel Razul, his daughter Tabina and a punk called Genghis."

Sherry, confused but excited by the mysterious behavior of her date, waited just out of earshot.

"Look, Hal, I've had enough warnings about Allah's Blade to recognize their leader when I see him. No, I don't know of any connection between the L.A. gang and Allah's Blade, but you can bet it won't be good."

Hal Brognola, Stony Man's contact with Washington, was responsible for sending Able Team, an elite antiterrorist group, into action. But this time Hal was having a problem getting excited about Ironman's sighting, although he knew that Carl's knowledge of the active terrorist file couldn't be ignored. He just couldn't let Able Team think it could jerk his chain at will.

"Okay, Carl, relax. I'll have one of our local contract men check out your concern. Do you have any more data?"

Ironman described the tall, skinny blond guy with the ponytail and the two-foot beard to Hal. He also had descriptions and license numbers for both cars.

"Thanks, Lyons. Go soak up some more sun, and a couple of smiles."

The blond warrior turned back to Sherry. "Where is that cave you wanted to see?"

"Just up and around that curve." She pointed. "By the way," she asked, sizing him up, "are you a bodybuilder?"

He pursed his lips and slowly looked her over. "No. I work out for my job. But it's obvious you're a bodybuilder." He cupped her dimpled chin in a callused hand. "And you're doing a good job of it."

4

The tournament between the highly contrasting opponents had reached the final round. The favorite, Abu, a Korean-trained Tang Soo Do black belt, stood patiently, waiting for Khalid to finish discussing his interpretation of the rules with the judges. Abu, built more like a tiger than a man, had fought this rich playboy before and had created a lifelong enemy.

"Next time!" the defeated major had yelled after his earlier loss to Abu.

"Is now the time?" Abu said quietly as his angry opponent signed in for the last round.

Major Omar Khalid was boiling. He had been training for just this bout since his humiliation. After his only defeat, Khalid had developed a full-blown obsession with destroying Abu. He'd taken leave to allow himself time to train under a different *sensei* in Rome. An advocate of Kempo karate, he still smarted when he remembered that Abu had publicly ridiculed him.

Kempo students, who concentrated heavily on hand movements, were often derided by other karate schools that favored leg techniques. Their unique manner of extending their arms and bringing both hands up and down did in fact resemble the motions of someone working with taffy.

"I demand that there be no limits to our techniques," said Khalid. "Is this a warrior's sport, or should we get a skirt for my alleged opponent?"

Both judges, who were local karate teachers, shook their heads. "Too dangerous," said the older of the two. "We don't want anyone killed; we just want to evaluate who has the best techniques."

Agitated, the handsome Arab pulled the older judge aside. "I have the authority to shut down every karate dojo in Libya. Either do it my way or dust off your passport." Knowing what the answer had to be, Khalid returned to the mat to warm up.

After a short conference, the senior judge walked slowly to the center of the mat and motioned both opponents to a spot in front of him. "It has been requested by Major Khalid that we cancel the rules in this bout." He couldn't look Abu in the eye. "What is your response, sir?"

Abu grinned. "Let the pouting child have his way. It will just mean he'll lose quicker." A split second before the official dismissed them, Abu held up his hand. "But I insist on one thing."

"Yes?"

In a voice loud enough to carry to the corners of the dojo, he said, "I want the match terminated and the championship awarded to me if my worthless enemy begs for mercy when the going gets rough."

In a movement too fast for most to see, Khalid launched a right backfist at Abu's head.

Abu had anticipated his enemy's attack. Chuckling, he caught the major's wrist and held it rigid. "Naughty, naughty."

In one silky move, the elder judge broke the hold and admonished the men to go to their corners.

No mats were used. Pieces of adhesive tape on the hardwood floor defined the corners of the fighting area. Both men stood, legs loose, shaking their arms. At the judge's hand signal, they walked to the center of the marked-off area. Abu bowed. Major Omar Khalid glared.

The crowd began to cheer for his opponent. "Abu, Abu, Abu..."

They circled, each assuming an attack position, then dropping it when the other took the proper defensive position. Gradually the typical opening stiffness disappeared from Khalid's movements, and he attacked with a round kick, followed by a hand technique to the head before retreating. Abu, suspecting an ambush, didn't follow.

He cocked his head and grinned. "Good stuff for a white belt."

Instead of losing his temper, as he had in their last match, Khalid ignored the taunt.

Stamping his right foot and then waiting for an answering movement, Abu settled in the center of the floor.

Khalid circled, shooting a side thrust kick at Abu's head.

Abu had expected the kick, and he blocked it with his forearm and reached for Khalid's ankle.

Delight flooded Khalid. This was a repeat of the way he'd lost the last bout. But his *sensei* in Rome had worked with him for a month to turn that failure into a victory. When Abu's left hand closed around Omar's ankle, he did not try to escape. Khalid placed another kick to Abu's jaw. It felt perfect, just the way he'd practised it.

The snapping of the Tiger's neck vertebrae could be heard throughout the entire dojo. Both judges leaped in to terminate the bout.

Abu collapsed, immediately losing control of all his bodily functions. His eyes rolled as he gasped for air.

With a shriek, Major Omar Khalid attacked the helpless lump. He delivered five straight blows to the dying man's head before the judges could control him.

Rage energized the crowd. They surged toward the mat.

Having anticipated their reaction to the loss of their hero, Khalid had stationed fifty of his men outside with instructions to enter when necessary. Within a minute of Abu's death, the major, still in his *gi*, marched out, surrounded by a cordon of his elite troops.

THE WELL-BUILT OFFICER in custom gabardines paced back and forth, reliving his victory. He addressed his image in a bronzed mirror.

"I'm more than a match for anyone who dares to challenge me." He grinned in approval of his speech.

A five-carat diamond sparkled on his right pinkie. Khalid also trained as a bodybuilder. His tailored shortsleeved shirt revealed slablike pectoral muscles and heavy triceps, both of which could only be acquired by spending hundreds of hours in a gymnasium.

Recently assigned to the Brotherhood as a liaison officer, he had quickly grown to hate the Berbers. He was politically influential in Libya. The officer waiting out in the foyer would suffer from his temper as everyone else did. Khalid believed that there was no one in the Brotherhood with the attributes necessary to lead him. It took extreme personal discipline to yield to higher-ranking officers. Khalid's next appointment had already waited an hour to report on his undercover assignment with Allah's Blade. When questioned about the waiting officer, Khalid had said, "Let the dog wait. I'll see that professional traitor when I'm ready."

Lieutenant Akmet, Allah's Blade's unknown mole, had a great deal of information to report when he was finally admitted.

From behind a ten-foot mahogany desk inlaid with verses from the Koran, Major Khalid sneered, "Why, Comrade Lieutenant Akmet, should I believe you? Do you speak for Allah's Blade?"

"No comrade, I speak for myself—and the Brotherhood."

Omar Khalid's eyes flashed, and he spun around. "Are you a traitor or a hero? How can I tell?"

Lieutenant Tariq Akmet met his glare without flinching. "Comrade major, I suggest you call General Mousa."

Within three minutes of the call, an orderly opened the door, admitting the heavyset man. Dressed in Berber robes, he wore crisscrossed bandoliers of 7.62 mm ammunition on his chest. He carried a battered FN-FAL, and he wore a magazine pouch. The bullet harness crossing his chest was outdated, but it reminded him of old desert battles and made him feel like a true warrior.

Both junior officers came to attention.

The general walked over to Lieutenant Akmet and kissed him on both cheeks.

Major Omar Khalid couldn't believe his eyes. He had thought his personal wealth and his influence with Khadaffi automatically made him the old man's favorite.

"What do you have for us, Tariq? I can't believe that maverick Razul has really come up with something valuable."

In great detail Akmet described Alonzo Black's bacteria to his imposing commander.

The major glared at the young man who was upstaging him.

Five minutes of silence followed the report as both junior officers waited for the general to speak.

"What rank are you, Tariq?" the general questioned finally.

"Lieutenant, sir. And, sir, I've been ordered to take two men and meet the colonel in California immediately."

"Hmmm." General Mousa glanced at Major Khalid and smiled.

"Well, Comrade *Major* Akmet, obviously I cannot promote you in Allah's Blade, but the Brotherhood appreciates your services. Please accept your new rank as our thanks. I suggest you continue with Allah's Blade and keep us updated. Major Khalid will take his Libyan team to the United States and relieve Allah's Blade of this wondrous new bacteria. He will be your contact."

He turned to Major Khalid. "Anything Tariq needs, give it to him. Anything. Thank you, comrades."

Mousa rose, and Khalid and Akmet stood, as well. Retrieving his FN-FAL, the general walked over to the new major and kissed him again and then stalked out.

The general didn't stop at his desk, but continued on to the Russian adviser's office. There he checked on his operation to back up both Allah's Blade and Khalid's team.

5

Rarely did Carl Lyons and his boss, Hal Brognola, disagree. Both had a kind of intuitive sense that pointed them toward trouble. Ever since he'd joined Able Team, the former L.A. cop had deferred to Hal. But this time the Ironman found himself vacillating between anger at the Fed and doubt about his own intuition. Still, he had to press the issue. It was like that last rep on a touch set of squats, when you felt the most inadequate and worked the hardest. He decided to talk to the other two members of the Team.

Sherry watched Lyons push his abalone steak around the plate. He was obviously totally preoccupied.

"Maybe it would be a good idea for you to take care of the problem before you starve to death," she suggested, chuckling.

Ironman jerked back to reality. "Problem? What problem?"

Pointing at Lyons with a fork, she said, "Yes, problem. I thought you were going to eat that phone back at the cove."

Lyons pulled on his lower lip.

Sherry rapped his knuckles with her fork. "'Fess up, Mr. Macho. You've got a problem, and until you take care of it I'm part of the woodwork. So why don't you fix whatever's broke and call me to celebrate when everything's glued back together?''

Lyons jumped to his feet with his usual finesse, knocking his chair over. He glanced at the check and threw a twenty and a ten on the table.

"Hold it, my blond stallion," laughed Sherry as she followed him out of the restaurant. "If you're going to call me, you'll need this." She handed him a slip of paper with several phone numbers on it. "It also has my Santa Barbara number. If you're still interested."

He pecked her on the cheek and sprinted toward the intersection of Prospect and Girard. "Thanks, babe," he yelled. "I owe you a champagne dinner at the Hotel Del Coronado."

During the short jog to the Casa sea wall, Lyons admitted to himself that Stony Man usually hit terrorist threats right on target. No detail was ignored by the secret counterterrorist group. Lyons knew that, but, damn it, even the great Hal Brognola could be wrong.

The Ironman arrived at the Casa de Mañana just as Blancanales, sunburned a fiery red, got out of his car.

"If you touch me I'll kill you," threatened Pol.

Ironman stopped and put his hands on his hips and laughed. "If you'll get that angry look under control, maybe I can get you a job advertising lobster—cooked lobster, that is."

"Real funny. What happened to that pretty young thing you hustled past here?"

"Never mind her, I've got a problem. Besides, she hustled me."

"Okay, Mr. Stud, but don't forget, sixteen can get you twenty—even in California. Anyway, what's the problem? Wait a minute. Here, put some of this on my back and legs, will you?'' Blancanales handed him a bottle of lotion.

Lyons took the bottle and carefully wrote the word *tourist* across his friend's shoulders. A passing local carrying a surfboard gave Lyons a grin and a thumbs-up sign. While slowly rubbing the oil over the sunburned former Black Beret, Lyons described his sighting and Hal's lukewarm response.

Living up to his nickname—"Pol," for "Politician"—Able Team's second member listened. Taking the tanning oil from Lyons, he nodded. "I know how you feel, but Hal has to challenge every bit of data he's presented, or he'd go off half-cocked sometimes. He probably already has the local contract agent checking on Allah's Blade."

GENGHIS DROVE down the side street toward Dnathro's head office. He rubbed his sore temple as he contemplated the day's events.

"I still don't see why you let that Anglo pig push us around," griped a heavily muscled Latino from the back seat.

Rubbing the tender spot on his left temple, his leader answered in a voice so soft the Latino had to lean forward to hear. "Because, man, our action is more important than getting busted for wasting an ex-cop in the middle of La Jolla." As he finished the sentence, Genghis swung his right elbow straight back into the Mexican's forehead, slamming him back into the seat. "Dig?"

Dazed, the Latino shook off the effects of the blow and muttered, "Dig, I dig, man," before clamping his lips.

Mok, the Horde's warlord, smiled. It was stupid to remind their leader that he'd been humiliated but, he mused, revenge was never more than a memory away.

Genghis looked in his rearview mirror at his Mongolian soldier. Nicknamed "Cuts Clean" but now called C.C., he was the toughest hood now carrying a knife. Stroking an Arkansas White whetstone with a fourteen-inch custom bowie knife, C.C. worked with the intensity of a diamond cutter.

"How we gonna work this action?" C.C. asked. "The cat in front has the juice and we're supposed to protect him, but we gotta deal with the Libyans to give them the bugs—it's getting complicated again." He took a small jeweler's loop from the pocket of his leather vest, positioned it in front of his eye and inspected the edge of his blade. "Getting there," he said. Then, remembering he'd asked a question, he took the magnifying glass out of his eye. "Well, boss, what's the action?"

"Like those cats who retire young from the military and then take a second job, we're double-dipping." Genghis laughed. "Colonel Razul and his Allah's Blade are paying us to back them up, and the Brotherhood's paying us to work for them when they take the bacteria away from Razul and his people."

The Horde's runner and point man struck the top of the front seat with his closed fist. "All right," he echoed. "Has old Genghis done it, man, or what?"

Mok, already in on the plans, nodded his approval while mentally continuing to go through his karate forms.

"Well, my man," continued Genghis, "I really haven't told you the whole story. Truth is—we're triple-dipping."

A chorus of "all rights" filled the Cad.

Encouraged by the cheers, the Horde's leader went on. "We get paid by Allah's Blade and the Brotherhood, and then, after taking the juice for ourselves, we're going to get paid by old Uncle Sam."

6

Once inside Dnathro, the group stopped to admire a ten-foot color-coded model of the famous double-helix DNA molecule. It swung gently from an arched ceiling, flashing multicolored lights giving it an eerie appearance.

"Looks like a corkscrew made out of colored marbles. Could be a copy of Mok's twisted brain. He's lost his marbles," C.C., gang comedian, commented.

Ignoring the humor and puffing out his chest, Alonzo Black waved his arm. "That's what it's all about, folks. A microsnip here, a little splice there, and—" he smiled at Colonel Razul "—you're rich."

For the first time, Razul and his men saw the maverick scientist as something other than a long-haired weakling.

"Does the bacteria you work with look like that?" asked Tabina.

Black, feeling more than adequate, patiently explained that the molecules for each bacteria had a different code that had to be dealt with by a number of techniques. He patiently explained enzyme snipping and gene splicing in the simplest of terms.

Then he made the same mistake that had forced him out of the doctoral program. Feeling superior, he reached out to pat Tabina's ass.

Unfortunately for Alonzo, Colonel Razul caught the movement. His head jerked up in shock. Before his daughter could respond, all his protective instincts exploded. Whistling between his teeth, he pushed her aside and grabbed the microbiologist by the right wrist. He pulled Alonzo toward him and placed the edge of his hand on the frightened traitor's elbow, slamming him to the floor.

The guard, who had remained at a respectful distance, turned his back to admire the DNA model.

Genghis watched, storing Razul's reaction away for future reference.

"The next time you insult the Razul family, I'll kill you, bacteria or no bacteria." The colonel then grasped the prone technician from behind, placing his thumb in Alonzo's armpit, his fingertips pressing on the meridian nerve. Immediately the microbiologist's breathing muscles went into paralysis.

Black started to suffocate.

Genghis watched, impressed.

"Father, please! Allah's Blade needs Mr. Black. We can punish him later."

Like a raging bull forced to pull up during a charge, Ziyad Razul put his anger on hold and massaged Alonzo.

"Get up, slime. The next time you insult my daughter you'll die more slowly than you thought possible."

The microbiologist, his face flat on the cold variegated-tile floor, refused to open his eyes. The reality of pain stunned him. Control, absolute control of his life, had never been wrested from him before. He'd always done whatever he wanted, consequences be damned, and he had never had to pay the bill in pain and fear.

Still whistling, the colonel grabbed him by the ponytail and jerked. "Get on your feet. Now."

Dignity gone, cheek still pressed to the floor, Alonzo pulled his knees up under his chin, grasped them and sobbed, "Stop, please, or I'll destroy the bacteria."

Quietly Tabina placed her hand on her father's arm and shook her head. He let go and drew his right index finger across his daughter's throat, pointing at the scientist with the other.

"Of course, father, of course." She tugged gently on his sleeve. "In time."

Unaware of Ziyad Razul's hand signals, convinced he was in control again, Alonzo opened his right eyelid, lessened his sobbing to sniffles and stood.

"You must know all about these places. Show me around," ordered Razul.

"Let's save some time," suggested their red-eyed captive. "Usually there are company brochures at the receptionist's desk describing the facilities."

Stacked next to the desk in an unopened bundle were hundreds of four-color handouts explaining the entire complex. The section on equipment had a layout of the technical area.

Colonel Razul handed him a copy. "Show the guard where we want to go."

Following the brochure's floor plan, they found the well-equipped labs. Alonzo Black whistled at the modern equipment. "This is going to be a piece of cake."

"Can you get started?" Razul asked.

"Just as soon as I recover my 'magic soup.'" Alonzo chuckled, enjoying his moment of importance.

"Well?" asked both Razuls at the same time. "When?"

"Let's talk about money."

"First the proof, then the money," countered the colonel.

"How do I know you'll pay?"

"Just a moment." Tabina walked over to confront the stubborn biologist. "We can satisfy both parties. I'll accompany Mr. Black to get his 'magic soup.' Here." She reached into her pocket and removed a bankbook and allowed the suspicious technician a peek. The first page had the name Alonzo Black printed on it and showed a balance of eight million dollars. It was forged, but it was good enough to fool an amateur. Tabina held it under his nose. "This is yours when you produce what you've claimed."

For the first time in as long as he could remember, Alonzo looked past a beautiful woman to read a book—a bankbook.

"We should go get my soup," he mumbled, visualizing himself smothered in naked women. "The mutated bacteria are in a locker in Carlsbad, not far from here."

"The Horde will back you up," promised the big Chinese, moving out.

FRANZ STRUDE LOVED living in San Diego but hated working there. Everything was too damned far apart. He couldn't get used to driving everywhere. He'd been raised in Stuttgart, Germany, and his old neighborhood had had everything a person could want—within walking distance. After coming to America he'd worked as a private investigator in New York, and again, except for the subways into the city, the boroughs were self-contained units. He'd lived in Queens. It was tough, but everything was only a subway ride away. But in San Diego only a trolley and a few infrequent buses represented what Californians called public transportation.

Shit, he thought. They needed a trip to the Big Apple to see how it was done.

Driving fifty miles a day represented a form of torture to Franz. He hated driving.

"But," he complained to the windshield, "I like the Fed's money." Glancing at his watch, he realized it had been an hour since he'd checked on the APB he'd conned the San Diego Police Department into putting out for him. He pulled into a Denny's restaurant and called the dispatcher.

"Hi, Gertrude, nine o'clock check, anything on my secure APB yet?"

"Just got a call from Northern. They spotted your yellow Mercedes in a cul-de-sac at the end of a street called Pipette."

"Thanks, babe. I owe ya."

"After dinner at the Cotton Patch tonight, you won't," she told him, chuckling.

"You got a deal. Gotta run. I'll call."

Ten minutes later, he arrived at Pipette Street. The dimly lit street would only help his recon. He had a war-surplus sniperscope that worked very well. Rather than risk getting trapped in a dead end, he decided to park and walk in, but before he could get out of his car the yellow Mercedes appeared and turned north.

Using his scope, Franz easily identified two of the suspects described by Brognola. I could follow that car anywhere, he thought as Tabina sped by. He waited until it disappeared around a corner, then slipped his Ford into gear. He didn't pick up the black Cadillac with its lights off that started up and shadowed him.

"Boss. Sweet Buns just picked up a tail," C.C. reported.

"I wonder who—? Shit," complained Genghis. "When you're dealing with ragheads, who can tell? Their idea of a clean mission is only seven double crosses."

"Well, Boss? What do we do?" C.C. asked.

Mok, who had been silent until then, chuckled and said, "Guess."

"Mok, take the driver. C.C., hit the car." Grinning as they checked their weapons, the Horde's best moved in silent obedience.

Strude, unaware of his tail, used his police radio, choosing a secure frequency. "Central, patch me into the watch commander." He waited for three minutes, keeping the yellow Mercedes in sight.

"Lieutenant Harris here."

"Harris, this is Strude, Franz Strude."

"What the hell are you doing on this frequency?"

"I'm on one of those spook follow-ups. Captain Gibbons approved the link. Check with the dispatcher."

"What the hell do you want?"

"Please call the number I left with the dispatcher, Gertrude. Tell the party I have a contact at Pipette Street and am following a car per their description on Highway 5. A young woman and a man with long hair and a ponytail heading north on Interstate 5. Hold it. I think—"

A burst from an AK-47 struck the rear quarter panel and stitched its way across the rear fender, ending by caressing the gas tank. The resulting explosion lifted the rear wheels off the ground and spun the car around so that the rear was pointing toward the yellow Mercedes. Within seconds the Ford burst into flames.

With the solid finesse acquired only by many hours of firing automatic weapons, Mok leaned into his AK, dispatching a controlled stream of death into the Ford's windshield. His shots were unnecessary.

The radio transmission stopped.

Mok smiled, placing his hand palm up where Genghis could see it.

The Horde's leader slapped it. "No medals for fun jobs, Mok."

Tabina and Alonzo watched the big orange ball of fire from the back seat of the Mercedes. Realizing for the first time what a heavy group he'd thrown in with, Alonzo stayed a mere gulp away from vomiting his fear all over the leather upholstery.

7

Lieutenant Akmet and two members of Allah's Blade landed at Lindbergh Field. Following instructions, they waited in front of the American Airlines terminal until a short, heavyset, bearded man in a blue Hawaiian shirt dropped his newspaper.

"Excuse me, sir, I believe you dropped this, this collection of tales," Akmet offered.

"True, too true," the contact answered, scratching his left elbow. It was the proper countersign. Without another word, the three Muslim terrorists joined the driver.

"I've rented you rooms at the Sentinel Hotel," he said. "It's between the lab and the airport."

"Have you contacted Colonel Razul yet?" asked Akmet. "What about weapons?"

"Colonel Razul is expecting you at the laboratory. I'll give you the address. As for weapons, check under your beds."

TABINA RAZUL and her frightened charge returned to the lab. Alonzo carried a foam-lined aluminum briefcase that contained two bottles of recombinant DNA—his so-called "magic soup." Immediately Tabina reported the explosion to her father.

"Did he survive?" Razul asked.

"Not a chance. Genghis took him out before he'd traveled a hundred yards. His car exploded. A good break, don't you think?"

"What about witnesses?"

She tilted her head and blew a cloud of smoke toward Alonzo. "Only *that*...and I'm sure he's not going to say anything. He knows he's an accomplice now." Wanting to intimidate Alonzo, they made no effort to hide their conversation from the biologist. He'd only live long enough to serve their purposes anyway.

All during the conversation, the technician was quaking. By the time they'd finished the debriefing, he was hyperventilating.

"Time is now a significant element," the colonel advised him.

Pointing at the terrified microbiologist with a glass tube she'd picked up, Tabina said, "That cupcake is pacing our mission. Maybe he needs special motivation."

"I have enough motivation," Alonzo interjected shakily. He paced, pulling on his beard. "The eight million you promised motivates the hell out of me."

Razul held one of the bottles of DNA between his thumb and index finger. "What would happen if I dropped this?"

Alonzo shrugged. "Nothing."

Shaking the flask as though he were mixing a cocktail, Razul squinted. "And what if I drank it?"

Without breaking his stride, the agitated biologist shot back, "Unless you had a gutful of oil, the same thing— nothing. How about my eight million?"

Lifting his eyebrows to hide his rising anger, the commander of Allah's Blade swallowed. "Five seconds after a successful demonstration."

"I'm tired of waiting."

Razul smiled. "One more question. Why do I need you now?"

"Because, colonel, if you tried to use what's in those bottles with the wrong procedure you'd kill all of my magic bugs."

Razul weighed the situation.

"I assumed we would need more of your formula. Do we have enough of this stuff to destroy a supertanker's cargo of oil?"

"No, for that amount I do need the lab," Alonzo answered. "And I'll need sixteen hours."

Razul dropped the bottle back into its polyurethane cavity. "Thursday we validate the bacteria, and if you have what Ibrahim Mohammet said you have, we'll pay." Tabina waved the forged bankbook.

Alonzo's head jerked up. He'd forgotten all about his friend.

"Where is Ibrahim? I expected him to come with you."

"Don't worry about him," Tabina said. "He wanted to visit his mother for a while. He did say to tell you hello."

"His share doesn't come out of mine," Alonzo said, wanting to confirm the deal.

"Of course not." Razul smiled. "My beloved nephew will be well taken care of by the family."

"Fine young man," purred Tabina. "I hope to be seeing him soon."

The lab door opened. "Lieutenant Akmet and two men reporting for duty, sir."

Colonel Razul acknowledged them, outlining the schedule. Immediately following a final run-through of the details, the three saluted and left.

FIVE WARRIORS SAT around the conference table at Stony Man Farm. All looked as though they were scheduled to bite the killing end off a firing .50-caliber machine gun. Ironman rubbed his knuckles, glancing around at the rest of Able Team. Blancanales combed his hair for the fourth time in as many minutes. Gadgets looked at his latest copy of *Electronics News* without seeing it. Cowboy Kissinger examined the blade of a five-inch boot knife and Aaron Kurtzman reread a printout while rocking his wheelchair.

It wasn't often the head Fed at the Stony Man facility lost his temper. When he did, everyone gave the bull a full pasture to run in. Back for only ten minutes, an apprehensive Able Team waited around the briefing table. They hadn't even unpacked from their West Coast holiday.

The door slammed open.

Hal Brognola's reluctance to act on Ironman's call had cost the life of one hell of a good man. Guilt as tangible as a hangman's sweat was smothering.

He snatched the file again. Opening it, he saw Razul's picture. He threw the folder onto the conference table.

Brognola shook his head twice to clear away the rage. "Ironman, we go to work. I want this one."

"You okay?" Pol asked, concerned.

"I'll be fine when Colonel Razul and his men get what they deserve."

Gadgets tried to lighten the mood. "I'll wire them for sound, and Lyons can—"

"Knock it off. Read." Hal handed briefing notes to the Able Team members. "The slides'll give you the rest. Roll it."

A complete dossier on Razul, Tabina and Akmet documented their ruthlessness. Pictures of three other members were included, but the data on them was minimal.

"As you have seen, Colonel Razul is a former military officer. Cashiered out of the Libyan army because he couldn't stand the restrictions. He fought the generals about targets and methods," said Hal.

"So he joined the Brotherhood and had the same problem," added Schwarz. "Went into business for himself, exercising a little free enterprise for our commie friends. They don't like mavericks."

"We just received an update from a CIA contact," continued Brognola. "Apparently Colonel Razul and Allah's Blade were refused additional funding by the Revolutionary Council. They have evaluated him as uncontrollable. He left the country with his daughter. It is assumed they are almost out of funds."

"That must be why they're here," Pol added, shifting to a position less painful for his sunburned back.

Brognola nodded, pursing his lips. "Yes, but that's not the scary part. The area and street where Franz Strude reported seeing them is heavily populated with genetic engineering firms."

"They could be involved in some germ warfare shit, couldn't they?" Carl Lyons asked, mentally picturing Able Team fighting in gas masks and protective clothing.

"Or they could be trying to acquire something to sell—if they're almost broke," Pol added. "That's an awfully small group for the Libyans. They normally like more clout."

Carl Lyons jerked upright in his chair. "Genghis. That must be the connection."

Brognola turned to Aaron Kurtzman, Stony Man's computer expert. "Do you have the printout on our mystery man?"

A printout lay on the Bear's lap. Confined to a wheelchair for the rest of his life, Kurtzman was a genius with a computer. The raid on Stony Man Farm by the KGB had left permanent scars on his body, but not on his mind.

"Let's check Ironman's past. We just look into this crystal ball, and what do we see?"

Lyons squirmed, frowning. With the palm of his hand he nervously pushed a pencil through the space in his closed fist.

"I see a cop assigned to East L.A. tangling with a group called the Hammer," Kurtzman said.

"Bastards, every one of them. Too bad they—" Lyons looked up and noticed that the computer expert was waiting patiently for him to shut up.

"Sorry."

Kurtzman grinned. "Bring back memories? Try these. After a gang war that included most of East L.A.'s turf, only a few clubs survived. The Hammer's leader, Bloody Chong, was slaughtered, hit in his front yard. Then his strong up-and-coming warlord took over by cutting his competitor's throat." He emphasized the last sentence with a finger drawn across his own throat and nodded his permission to Lyons to comment.

"Genghis. I knew that he'd slit Chong's throat, but I couldn't prove it. We tangled plenty after that. He even tried taking me out with a bomb. Couldn't prove that, either."

Brognola pursed his lips. "Smart?"

"You bet. Warlord at seventeen ain't chopped liver. He dug history, and he laid out the most sophisticated battle plans the department had ever seen. In fact, that's what put most of the heat on him. Whenever we ran into a complicated plan we'd head for Genghis.''

"Can you give us an example of how his head works? If we tangle, it might help the others to anticipate him.''

"Sure." Ironman's face contorted as he searched his memory bank for a good example. He tapped the metal end of the pencil against his teeth.

Gadgets laughed. "Ironman's mind just rusted out.''

Flipping his pencil at him, Lyons snapped, "At least I have one to rust.''

"Testy, testy," Gadgets kidded him.

"Okay. This is a typical Genghis maneuver. We suspected that he planned on picking up a delivery of cocaine from Mexicali, Mexico. From there the shipment entered L.A. via Riverside, California. We knew the route but held up on the bust, wanting to nail the Hammer. We tailed the driver to a small unoccupied house in the suburbs, where he parked the car in a garage and left. My men wanted to move in, bug the house and put a beeper on the car.''

"Sounds logical," said Gadgets, who was always interested in putting little electronic insects to work.

"Two things bothered me. One, the house might be under observation, and two, Genghis might have it booby-trapped.''

"So did you just join the watchers?" asked Blancanales.

Lyons glanced down, rubbing the table with his right hand. "Nope, I outflanked him. I phoned the next-door neighbors and convinced them to vacate and go to a motel for a couple of days.''

"Good move," the Bear offered.

"Bad move," countered Ironman. "Bad, bad move.''

Carl pursed his lips, squeezing the unhappy memory out. "The neighbors' porch had already been booby-trapped. With a radio-activated bomb. They blew two of my team away."

"The bastard does think ahead, doesn't he?" Brognola said.

"We called in the bomb squad."

"And?" Pol knew more was coming.

"The Hammer had bugged three more houses—and the car, which we found to be clean. Not as much as a marijuana seed anywhere."

"Not only smart, but mean," Brognola summarized.

"So much for history. What's his gang up to lately?" Gadgets asked.

Aaron picked up his printout. "First of all, he's changed the name of his gang from the Hammer to something more fitting. Now he calls them the Horde—the Mongol Horde. Here's a possible connection. They've been subcontracting muscle to the Libyans."

"Shit, I should have pulled his fucking arm out when I had it," Ironman muttered. "Allah's Blade and Genghis working the same problem— We've got a load."

Kurtzman handed the computerized information to Carl Lyons. "You can study this while you're flying out to the Coast."

"Time to hit the road," Ironman ordered.

"Except maybe we should issue Blancanales an umbrella if we're going back to southern California." Schwarz laughed.

If there was anyone who didn't need lessons on living in a warm climate, it was Rosario Blancanales. A veteran of the Vietnam war, he had earned his "bones" as a point man with the Black Berets. His tours in the jungles had exposed him to every survival situation a warrior might have to adjust to. Since the formation of Able Team, he had added more combat experience than the real Genghis Khan had known. None of which had kept him from getting badly sunburned after falling asleep on a beach in La Jolla.

"I may need an umbrella, but I'd suggest someone check out the birth certificate of Lyons's date," Pol said. "She dropped her teething ring when he patted her on the rump."

"Don't pat either Razul or his daughter," Brognola cautioned. "They are both experts in a form of kung fu seizing art. You pat that deadly little sweetie and you might die."

"What do you mean, seizing?" Lyons asked.

"About thirteen hundred years ago the Chinese martial arts people learned all about the meridian nerve paths that acupuncture doctors use. Only they use pressure on them to paralyze and kill."

"Do we have anything on the string bean I saw with Tabina?" the Ironman asked, changing the topic.

"Not a thing. Zip."

"Looks like right now our best bet is to pick up where Strude left off," Gadgets offered. "Maybe a little electronic surveillance?"

Cowboy Kissinger, Stony Man's weapons expert, spoke up. "Let's consider this kung fu crap these terrorists use. I think we should evaluate the need for an additional weapon, an ankle piece, maybe."

"What the hell's wrong with my Beretta 93-R?" Pol asked. "It shoots things up close."

Schwarz laughed. "We have enough trouble now keeping Blancanales from shooting himself in the foot. If he had an ankle gun I think I'd worry."

"As usual, our electronics genius has blown a fuse. Someone show our demented friend where the ankle is located. Besides, he's been staring into his oscilloscopes for so long he couldn't find his weapon unless it had a knob and a screen."

"All right, guys, hold it for a moment," Lyons said. "What's the logic behind the extra weapon?"

"If this martial art is as deadly as it sounds, we should anticipate being in trouble with it."

"Trouble?" Pol asked.

"Sure. Able Team is always working up close. This is a hands-on kind of fighting style. Being able to access a weapon from an unexpected place may give you an edge. It's optional, of course."

Ironman had never carried a hideaway, but he knew he couldn't pass up any edge. "I'll go for it," he said. "What peashooter do you recommend?" When it came to weapons, the Ironman preferred cannons—Magnum cannons.

"I rejected the smaller calibers, .22 through .32. When you consider that an opponent's hand pressure could kill you, I wouldn't try discouraging anyone with something smaller than a .38."

"Got a brand in mind?" Lyons asked.

"Yup, the Smith & Wesson Bodyguard. It has a shrouded hammer. In an emergency you don't need your weapon hanging up in your pant cuffs."

Gadgets laughed. "By the time we get to San Diego, Rosario will have trouble keeping his ankle piece from hanging up on his peeling skin."

8

A tall, agitated police lieutenant paced back and forth in the baggage claim area. Finally he spotted Lyons. "Ironman!"

Carl Lyons froze. Not many people, and only a few friends, called him that.

In his haste to get to Lyons, Lieutenant Harris bowled over a Navy boot returning from his first leave. "Sorry, buddy, didn't see you."

The swabbie, happy to see that the man hurrying past him was a uniformed police officer, breathed a sigh of relief.

Lyons balanced himself on the balls of his feet, just in case. Gadgets and Pol flanked him, standing in front of their war bags.

"You seem to be ever so popular." Gadgets chuckled. "We've only been on the ground for five minutes and you have a reception committee."

"Harris, San Diego PD. Glad to see you guys."

Now he had everyone's attention.

Flashing his most charming grin, Pol moved the noisy lieutenant away from the baggage retrieval belt. "Let's not make it too obvious. Okay?"

"Sorry," he answered in a stage whisper and with a slight duck of his head.

He shook all three men's hands. "You have no reason to know me, but I was involved in the operation that got Franz Strude killed."

Looking around to see if anyone could still hear the loud officer, Lyons asked, "How?"

"I was in contact with Strude on the radio, probably just as he bought it. I looked further into his assignment. He'd explained his job to Captain Gibbons, so I was briefed."

"Tight-mouthed bastard, wasn't he?" Blancanales grumbled. "Did you get the sizes of our shorts?"

"What can you tell us about Strude's death?" Lyons asked.

"Not much, except that he was taken out by a pro. His car blew from a gas-tank hit. Not much left—part of his skull and his feet."

"Find anything strange? Any witnesses?" continued the Ironman.

"We did have a single report of someone seeing a big black car driving with its lights out, but no confirmation. That's about it," concluded Harris. "Oh, yes. Captain Gibbons asked me to offer our services while you're in the area."

"Thank you very much," Pol said. "There is one thing that will be of great help. Could you get us a rundown on all of the businesses on a street called Pipette?"

"As quickly as possible," promised Harris. "Where will you be staying?"

"At the La Jolla Sentinel," said Gadgets. "Registered as Johnson, Klein and Talamantez." He didn't think it necessary to inform Harris that they had learned that Allah's Blade had checked into the hotel by tapping the Bear's computer into the FBI's immigration data.

Lyons stepped in front of Lieutenant Harris just as he was about to leave. "How did you recognize me, and where did you get my nickname? I'm sure Strude didn't know it."

"I guess you didn't recognize Captain Gibbons's name. He worked with you in the East L.A. strike unit for a week. He has a colorful description of you, right down to your Python."

Lyons couldn't put a face to the name.

"Naw, it was the warrior look of your handsome jaw that did it," Schwarz told him. "Harris knows a man of steel when he sees one."

Chuckling, the police officer shook hands all around and left.

The bantering continued for the rest of the time it took them to rent cars and drive to their hotel. On the way, Gadgets and Rosario decided that, as a minimum, Ironman should wear a red cape and have a red *S* sewn on all his shirts.

Lyons, a little tired of their endless badgering, snorted. "If you don't stop tugging on my cape you just might find your lips clamped by some outside force."

Blancanales and Schwarz, realizing they might have jerked his cape a time too many, rolled their eyes and shut up.

The Sentinel looked like many of southern California's hotels; it was a giant three-story motel sprawling out over five acres. Palm trees, undoubtedly put there for the tourists, thrust their green hands up near every entrance. The hotel's lobby was just as distinctive. Travel posters from the South Pacific fulfilled all of the decorator's needs in the way of tropical atmosphere. A topless plaster Hawaiian mannequin in a grass skirt, the tip of her nose and one of her nipples knocked off, greeted them.

As he passed, Gadgets rubbed the healthy nipple for luck.

Pol laughed. "Kid's never been weaned."

When they checked in, Lyons insisted on one room facing an elevator lobby and two more on the opposite wall. Pretending to be afraid of fire, Pol conned the desk clerk into putting them on the second floor.

"Let's have a cup of coffee and peruse the map. It'll give us a better understanding of the area," suggested Gadgets. "If we locate our target street, maybe we can put one of my little eavesdropping devices on a car."

The hotel restaurant was empty except for a single waitress and a wet off-duty dishwasher with swollen, water-soaked hands who was trying to put the moves on her.

"C'mon, baby," he pleaded, loud enough for all to hear. "Gimme a break." He stopped to light a soggy cigarette.

"Get lost, creep."

The butt flared and went cold. The dishwasher glared at the smoldering end and threw the stub at the coffee urn. "Shit." He reached for another, then grabbed the waitress by the upper arm. She pulled away.

"Get away from me or I'll—"

"You'll what? Turn me in to my brother? He'll fire your ass." The dishwasher rubbed his tattooed arm. "It's me, baby, or the unemployment line."

Suddenly pain enveloped his entire body. "W-what the—?" He twisted to find the source of the pain.

Closing a steel-hard grip around the punk's neck, a cold-eyed blond man lifted him up even with the hardest eyes the dishwasher had ever seen. Carl Lyons squeezed a little harder and whispered, "Shut your mouth. The lady asked you to leave." He set the shaking stranger back on his stool.

In one motion, the punk leaped off the stool and disappeared into the kitchen.

"Thanks, mister," the waitress said. "It gets a little old."

Lyons nodded and rejoined the group to a chorus of cheers. Ignoring a Please Wait to Be Seated sign, they took a booth next to a window and ordered. Ironman ordered grapefruit juice, the others coffee.

"Mr. Healthy," Schwarz said, "is afraid that coffee will rust the Ironman."

Lyons, instead of replying, stiffened, then nodded in the direction of three men who had just come into the restaurant. Instantly, Able Team shifted from banter to badass. Lieutenant Akmet and two other Middle Eastern men, obviously carrying, were following the hostess to their table.

The Politician quickly grabbed three menus from the next booth. Johnson, Klein and Talamantez disappeared behind the improvised barriers. When Allah's Blade began ordering, Klein and Talamantez slipped out, leaving Ironman behind.

Talamantez, with a twenty, convinced the eager desk clerk that he was part of a welcoming committee for his Arab friends. Their California relatives wanted to surprise the trio with a little party in their rooms. Always anxious to make an extra buck, the clerk responded by giving him the room numbers. After thanking him, Talamantez headed up to the third floor and the Blade's operational base.

Klein went back to the restaurant to give Ironman the room numbers. "Ring once if they leave here and twice if they take the elevator," he instructed Lyons.

"See what firepower we're facing. Bug 'em, if possible."

Able Team's electronic genius smiled. "One of the family's aggressive little insects is liable to attach itself to anything—a telephone, even. I've got to find Aunt Mabel. See you at the zoo at ten," he said in a loud voice as he turned and left.

Pol's lock-picking skills gained him quick entry. The room was neat, with only one suitcase lying open on the bed. A quick search revealed nothing. There was an unfolded road map with the way to the hotel marked in red, obviously the work of the car rental agency. Blancanales looked for more markings. Pipette Street was marked in pencil. Three soft knocks alerted him to Gadgets's arrival.

"Anything worth seeing?" Schwarz asked.

Bending to check under the bed, Pol shook his head. Then he whistled softly. "Look."

Three AK-47s were lined up on the floor, with five red plastic double magazines beside each one. Frag grenades rested in a deadly cluster, and two boxes of 9 mm parabellum FJ ammunition lay alongside. "At least they're neat," Pol said admiringly.

"Looks like our friends want to play cops and robbers," Gadgets stated, reaching into his electronic goody bag. "I'm going to try something new." He took a screwdriver and removed the butt plate from the stock of one of the Kalashnikovs. With a small gouge he hollowed out a space big enough for one of his custom transmitters. One by one he buried his nosy little friends in the terrorists' AK-47s.

"Maybe one of these direction finders will call out to Daddy," said Gadgets. "Let's add a couple of voice transmitters." In two minutes he had placed them in the base of the phone and under the towel rack in the bathroom. "Never know what kind of conversations will occur while shaving." As an afterthought, he added one more in the phone receiver, where it could be easily found. "Amateurs usually stop at one," said Schwarz, hoping these guys weren't too smart.

He hung up the phone. It immediately rang twice and then stopped.

"That's for us," warned Gadgets, brushing the last of the shavings from his work on the rifles onto a piece of hotel stationery. "Let's go."

They let themselves out, walking casually away from the area. They were not fast enough, however, as they were spotted by one of the trio.

The smallest terrorist, puzzled, stopped and said, "Tariq, wasn't he the man in the restaurant who said he was going to the zoo?"

Pol, deciding that maybe he and Gadgets had been noticed walking too close to the Blade's headquarters, moved to confuse them. He snapped his fingers and turned to face them. "Excuse me, sir," he said to Tariq. "We were to meet our family at a place called the San Diego Zoo. Could any of you gentlemen possibly give us directions? We've lost the map the car rental agency gave us."

Taken back, Akmet shook his head. "We're strangers here ourselves."

Pol wouldn't let him turn toward his room. "Oh, is that right? We're from Florida. Where you folks from? Talamantez here. My friend's name is Klein."

"Klein, Harry Klein," Gadgets said, sticking his hand out. "After we get through with the family we're going to party a little." He closed his eye in an exaggerated wink. "You wouldn't happen to know any pretty young—"

"No!" blurted Tariq. "Excuse me, but we have many obligations. If you will excuse us. Please." He turned to leave.

Gadgets reached for his arm. "Well, buddy, if you change your mind, we're in room 242. You're welcome to join the party. It starts at twelve or so."

"Goodbye, sir," one of the other terrorists said, turning away. The three men hustled toward their rooms to get away from the party boys.

"Midnight!" Gadgets, biting his lips to keep from roaring, yelled, "It starts at midnight!"

The last gunsel glared at the pair as they closed the door.

"Let's go hear what they're up to," Gadgets said. "I'm recording their blabber."

Ironman turned the corner and saw the chuckling warriors. "What was that all about?"

"My friend Harry Klein is just a little too aggressive for our friends from Allah's Blade."

"DECADENT BASTARDS," spit the youngest of Tariq's group. "All they ever think about is entertaining themselves." He kicked a chair.

Leaning, his back to the door, and his hand still on the doorknob, Lieutenant Akmet frowned, pursing his lips. He shook his head. Under his breath he muttered, "Something's wrong."

Both of the younger men went silent.

"Sir?" asked the chair-kicker.

Tariq gripped his chin and stroked his jaw with his fingertips. "They're phonies."

Both men, knowing they had missed something, watched Akmet.

"If those men were going to meet someone at the zoo and their room is 242, it's on the other side of the elevator. What were they doing walking away from our rooms and the elevator?" He pointed at both men, placing his index finger over his lips. He reached the phone in one stride and unscrewed the mouthpiece. The microminiature bug fell out.

Still holding his index finger on his lips, Akmet bent over and picked it up. He motioned to one of the others to turn on the TV. Once it was on, he pointed upward, instructing them to increase the volume. He guided both men to the bathroom after placing the bug gently on the floor in front of the set.

After shutting the door, he whispered, "I want you two to neutralize these CIA dogs. Hit them in their room. Now. Once you gain access, execution will be easy. I'll back you."

Able Team listened to the plans coming in over the bug Gadgets had placed under the towel rack.

"Looks like we're going to have company," mused Lyons, automatically checking his Python. He shook his head, pulling his coat down over the holster. "It's got to be quiet."

"A silenced Beretta 93-R only coughs occasionally," Pol offered.

"I've got his brother," added Gadgets. "Two 93-Rs ought to be able to handle those lightweights. We'll set 'em on three bites per trigger pull."

Ironman shook his head. "Never consider anyone a lightweight if he's willing to create a killing zone with you at the center. I do think it would be better to take them out somewhere other than inside the hotel.''

''That may be up to them. If they make too big a ruckus they'll never be able to get their hardware out,'' Pol said.

A knock on the door and a telephone call at the same time accelerated the action.

Pol slipped into the bathroom, leaving the door open a crack, and Gadgets took a position just around a corner in front of a bed.

''Hello, 242 here,'' Lyons said, answering the phone.

''Johnson?''

''Yup. Harris?''

Able Team's guests burst into the room, 9 mm Browning ACPs scanning, and spotted Ironman talking on the telephone.

''Hang up,'' ordered the smaller of the two intruders. ''Now.''

Lyons shrugged. ''Got a visitor. Call back in five minutes.'' He hung up.

The slighter terrorist moved forward. ''Where are the other two dogs?''

''At the zoo with Aunt Mabel.''

''Liar,'' the gunman snarled, pointing his weapon at Ironman's chest and tightening his finger on the trigger.

''Careful,'' admonished the Able Team commando.

The lead terrorist grinned, not knowing that the word *careful* signaled the release of Able Team thunder.

Gadgets stepped out and Pol opened the door as the command word triggered combat speed.

The heavier of the Libyan strike team turned toward the bathroom in time to see the biting end of Pol's Beretta cough three 9 mm telegrams. It caught the invader dead center in the sternum, exploding his heart. His eyes said, "Nobody told me it hurt this much to die," and then closed.

"One down," Pol said to himself as he turned to assist Schwarz. There was no need.

Gadgets moved out, confronting his adversary.

The slight attacker froze, his weapon still pointed at Lyons. He felt as though someone had welded his shoulders to his arms, then hung a weight on each of his hands. All he could move were his eyes. Only the whites were visible to Ironman as the killer focused on the end of Gadgets's silencer. He was trying to fire at Lyons, but his mind couldn't process killing and dying at the same time.

He received all the help he needed with his dilemma. The first three rounds from Schwarz's silenced Beretta entered the side of the man's confused brain and then exited, taking his hatred and his communist doctrine with him. The red spray on the wall testified to Gadgets's second talent. Extermination. The next three rounds weren't needed.

Killing came harder to Gadgets than electronics. Somehow it seemed to Schwarz that he'd been born with an oscilloscope for a brain. As he'd grown up a computer had joined the scope in his head. When he was just thirteen he'd badgered a local electronics firm to let him sweep the floors in an R and D laboratory that designed miniaturized transmitters and receivers. Before long the staff had recognized his natural bent for dealing with abstract problems, and they'd hired him as a part-time trainee.

At first, most of his duties involved sorting parts and soldering simple breadboard circuits for the engineers. Before long, the patient explanations of feedback, cross talk, amplifiers, filters and radio frequency techniques began to bear fruit. Most of the staff knew the skinny boy as "the kid." Schwarz didn't care what they called him, as long as he could continue to work at the firm. And it didn't even matter that not everyone wanted him there. He remembered the time Joe had tried to get rid of him.

"Hey, kid. This breadboard you just finished is a little noisy. How about using your spooky nose to find the reason?" Harry, the senior circuit designer, asked. "Find it before three and I'll have Joe sweep the floors for you. He couldn't solve the problem."

Within thirty minutes "the kid" located the marginal transistor and two wires that were placed too close to each other.

Harry laughed. "Joe, find the broom. The kid's done it again."

Stung by the pimple-faced boy's skills, Joe vowed to ride the teenybopper out of the lab. Three times the kid had rubbed his nose in a mistake. The boss refused to acknowledge that Joe had too much to do. It smarted to have that untrained brat show him up. But talent beat ego, and the boy survived. Schwarz absorbed everything the senior designers passed under his nose.

"Well, kid, you've done it again," Harry announced.

"W-what have I done this time?" the young man asked, nervous because of the mishaps around the shop that had been attributed to him.

"Don't get nervous, kid. This is a compliment."

"Compliment?" Gadgets rolled a tweaking tool around in his fingers.

"This is the cleanest microminiature receiver this lab's ever produced."

"Honest sir, I just relayed out the printed circuit-board to minimize the cross talk. It's Joe's design."

Harry lowered his voice to a whisper. "Bullshit, kid. This is your work."

Gadgets Schwarz was a technical sponge who sucked up every bit of new data available—until Nam. When he met communist brutality for the first time, an awareness, a realization of the need for his skills in the battle against the treacherous scums of the world, hardened him. Then came Able Team, and the need to combine his technical genius and the lessons Nam had taught him.

Lyons glanced at his watch. Less than fifteen seconds had passed since they'd been attacked. "Four and a half minutes till Harris calls back. Time for Johnson, Klein and Talamantez to check out."

9

Everyone in the old Sikorsky flying banana held tightly on to their own thoughts. The *whump* of the blades, competing with the engine noise, limited any type of conversation. The relic had been cheap, even if both the copter and its red-nosed World War II pilot had seen better days.

Both claustrophobic and afraid of heights, Alonzo sat hunched over in his seat with his knees up around his chin. He refused to open his eyes or take his hands off his ears.

Razul nudged his daughter and nodded toward the terrified microbiologist. "Let's hope we don't have to deal with that coward much longer."

"Twenty-four hours from now we should know," Tabina assured him.

Pointing out the open hatch at a line on the horizon, Akmet interrupted their discussion. "There it is, sir."

The VLCC (Very Large Crude Carrier) *R. P. Zinglow* looked like a huge crocodile lying in wait for innocent prey. Over eleven hundred feet in length, the supertanker filled the horizon as the Sikorsky flew nearer.

"Dig that awesome mutha," gasped C.C.

"I dig, man," whispered Mok. "That's some kinda rowboat, man."

"Be cool. Be cool," ordered Genghis. "That's not a ship. That is—" he pulled an imaginary trigger "—our killing ground."

A Libyan-registered ship with a crew of thirty-two mixed nationals and a Lebanese captain, *R. P. Zinglow* carried 250,000 tons of Iranian crude. Originally destined for the Come By Chance tanker facility in Newfoundland, Canada, she'd become a pawn in the game of high finance and had been rerouted from Japan to the northeast coast. Held for alleged turbine repairs off the coast of California, she would finally be underway again once the "team of scientists" had come aboard.

After the team landed, Colonel Razul met the captain and confirmed that their task was to sample oil from each of the main holding tanks. The skipper assigned four of the crew to assist them.

"We'd like to start forward, next to the bow, and work our way back to the bridge," Razul requested.

Section by section, they went through the motions, taking a small amount of crude and depositing an open container of Alonzo Black's mutated bacteria. They were finished in two hours.

Genghis and two soldiers leaned against a hose derrick and watched.

"When do we hit the crew?" C.C. asked.

"The minute we get a signal they've got the last hold doctored," Genghis answered.

"What do these cats have to gain by wasting a whole crew?" one of the soldiers questioned. "Why not just poison the oil and split?"

Genghis, watching Mok and a terrorist scouting the bridge and the crew quarters, answered, "Publicity, man. Once a shipload of ruined cargo is found with a dead crew, the media will kill each other trying to give Razul's bugs international attention.''

"Attention? Won't that bring the Feds down on our heads?'' asked the Mongol.

Mok signaled that everything was okay.

Responding with a nod, the confident gang leader told C.C., "Sure, the Feds will be after the murderers, and we'll give them to those hardworking Feebies.'' He pointed at the trio finishing the last hold. "Besides, with worldwide coverage, the price of the bacteria goes up.''

All the members of the scientific team met just under the bridge wing, where their equipment bags had been set.

Colonel Razul signaled for silence. "Is the Horde ready?''

Genghis nodded.

They rechecked their watches.

"The captain has agreed to give us a tour of the ship. Drop off in each area as we agreed, and strike at 1400. Remember, this is total annihilation. I want thirty-two corpses. Thirty-two.''

Razul again signaled for silence as the ship's senior officer approached. The man's obvious admiration for Tabina did not go unnoticed.

"Captain Mustafa, how kind of you to take time to show us your ship,'' she purred, taking the stocky officer's arm.

Mustafa beamed and led Allah's Blade's most dangerous member into the superstructure.

By the time they reached the bridge, only Tabina and her father remained with the captain. Taking his right hand in hers, she applied lethal pressure to the tiger's-mouth part of his hand. The confused officer slipped to the floor. He clutched his chest, straining like an asthmatic to breathe. His color darkened to purple and he died reaching toward Tabina's ankle.

At the same time, another Horde member threw two frag grenades into the crew quarters. The three off-duty men sleeping in their racks never even heard the explosions.

In the galley, C.C. swung his fourteen-inch custom bowie in an arc, slitting the throat of the ship's cook, then turned and slashed his youthful assistant. Falling across a chopping block, the young Greek died trying to stanch the flow of blood pulsing from the gap. Neither of the men had sensed that their lives were in danger when C.C. had entered the room.

Two other galley workers grabbed butcher knives to defend themselves with.

"What the hell—?" a slight Lebanese asked, shaking with terror.

"Fuck this," an older Italian yelled. "Run, kid!"

Before either of them could move, the stocky Mongolian blocked them and swung his bloody weapon at the boy's wrist.

"Allah help me," the boy cried out when he saw his hand lying on the deck. He fainted, blood pumping from his wrist.

"Son of a bitch," the old man yelled. "Just a kid." He charged, his butcher knife held high.

C.C. sidestepped and plunged his knife into the Italian's chest.

The old man's weapon clattered on the steel deck. "Bastard" was the last word to escape his lips.

Humming an old Chinese melody, C.C. leaned over and cut the unconscious boy's throat.

Seconds before the hit was to go down Mok shoved the door to the dining room open and smiled. Two of the seven men eating at the table motioned for him to have a seat. The Horde's warlord smiled back and brought his Uzi SMG up, returning their hospitality with a stream of instant death. It happened so quickly and was so unexpected that the unarmed men didn't stand a chance. Two chairs away was the farthest any of them scrambled before being cut down.

In the engine room, Akmet was struggling. The ship's engineer, a balding Cypriot, had witnessed the killing of four of his shipmates and hidden. As Akmet backed out of the room, the sailor slipped out from behind the fuel lines and battered him to his knees with a four-foot piece of rusty pipe. Only extreme concentration kept Akmet from passing out.

In his hurry to finish the killer, the engineer slipped and fell. Before he could gain his feet, Akmet had recovered. He stitched a row of red Kalashnikov kisses across the mechanic's white T-shirt. The angry Cypriot died reaching for his murderer.

Racing up and down the passageways with frag grenades, another Horde soldier was having a field day. Room after room exploded into orange-and-red flames before the startled crew members could escape. Only two men made it into the passageway before being cut down.

After killing the navigator and the helmsman, Razul and his daughter returned to the helicopter. The Horde members were congregating under the bridge wing, where they picked up their weapon bags.

Mok finished his body count, signaling toward the derrick with a thumbs-up and a nod.

The Horde and Akmet moved to follow Genghis to the aircraft. When they arrived, both Razul and his daughter motioned for the men to look inside.

Curled into a tiny ball, Alonzo Black held the top of his head with both hands and sobbed.

"It's time to get out of here," Razul ordered, pointing at the pilot.

GADGETS'S DIRECTION FINDER agreed with Lieutenant Harris's guess. Dnathro was the base of operations for Allah's Blade. Two of his microminiature bugs were chirping with a comforting regularity, and by using the portable DF he had zeroed in on the building.

"There. There's a guard on his rounds," Lyons pointed out. "They must be on a mission. I don't think they'd leave the rest of their equipment behind without some kind of a watch."

"One way to find out," Blancanales said, checking his Beretta 93-R.

Lyons pointed at Pol. "Cover the back. Gadgets, you take the front with me."

"Wait a minute," Pol said. "Why don't I just knock on the front door and ask when the building will open for business?"

Lyons and Schwarz grinned at each other. It was so obvious that neither of them had thought of it.

"Okay, I'll cover the rear," Lyons ordered. "Gadgets, back up Rosario."

After getting into position, the Ironman clicked the switch on his radio twice to signal *Go*.

Three minutes after Blancanales knocked on the window, the guard appeared. He pulled a curtain aside and shook his head, mouthing the words "Not open." He had the flap on his holster unbuttoned.

"Careful," Gadgets whispered, monitoring his DF. "One of our bugged AK-47s moved when you knocked."

Rosario Blancanales functioned as Able Team's public relations man. Even during his tours in Nam he had demonstrated an unusual ability to communicate with anyone.

The big grin on the Politician's face convinced the guard that he was just some harmless nut looking for a lost friend. The man opened the door a crack.

"Good morning, sir," said Pol. "I'm looking for Dr. Isaac Fluten. I was told he worked here."

Easing his right hand away from his weapon, the guard shook his head. "Nobody by that name here. You must have the wrong company."

Rosario bit his lip in mock frustration. "I'm sure he works here. Maybe he's on some kind of leave. Could I use your telephone, sir?"

Impressed by this polite, well-dressed man who was treating him like a person, the guard hesitated, then pushed the door open. "On the receptionist's desk, but don't leave the lobby."

When the guard turned, Gadgets slipped up and placed the whispering end of his Beretta at the base of his skull. "Both hands behind your head and lock your fingers before kneeling."

Rosario clicked his radio on. "Johnson, groceries have been bagged. Please pick up at front counter."

"Who are you," the guard questioned. "CIA?"

"Let's just say that we're concerned Americans," Pol explained, slipping the S & W .38 out of the kneeling man's holster.

"I'm going to look around to see what the hell we have here," Gadgets announced as he scanned with his DF. "Talk to me. Keep on chirping, baby."

The look on the guard's face reflected his opinion that Schwarz was a psychopath.

Pol caught the puzzled expression. "He's just a fun guy with wires, transistors and microchips instead of a brain. On your face and spread your arms and legs before I turn you over to him."

Carl Lyons chose that moment to enter through the front door. "Who's our friend?"

Blancanales shrugged. "Someone who thinks we're CIA."

"I'm sure he can admit to more than that," the Ironman said, kneeling and pointing his Python .357 Magnum at the guard. Lyons moved the hammer to half cock so that the weapon wouldn't fire. He slowly pulled the trigger until the knuckles of his index finger turned white.

From the dying end of a Python, there's no way to tell the cannon won't roar. Sweat beads formed on the prone man's forehead. The Carlsbad communist cell had assured him that he would only have to play guard for a week. It was supposed to be a nice easy job—no pressure. And now he was looking down the business end of a deadly weapon.

"What do you want?" he whispered.

"Where are Colonel Razul and Genghis?"

The guard counted the indentations on the Python's cylinder. "They've gone to test the bacteria on a supertanker."

"What bacteria? Talk to me," Lyons demanded.

The guard managed to relate the bits and pieces he knew about Dr. Alonzo Black and his mutated bacteria.

"Shit," Ironman exclaimed. "What if he's telling the truth? If that bacteria gets into the hands of the terrorist community, the repercussions could be staggering. Oil-field destruction will be the name of the game."

"We only have one option: we must neutralize all of the bacteria and the source when we strike," Pol said.

"How long have they been gone? When do you expect them back?" Lyons demanded.

"They've been gone four hours. Due back within two," the emotionally exhausted man answered in a whisper.

"What do they plan on doing after the test is over?" Lyons asked, continuing the interrogation.

"Contact more Libyans for a possible sale."

Schwarz returned with two AK-47s. "These are two of the three we saw up at the hotel. I found one just around the corner." Then he asked offhandedly, pointing toward the guard, "What'll we do with him?"

The terrified guard looked up at each of the men. "Please, I'll do anything you ask. I'll stay on the job and report to you. Please don't kill me."

Lyons frowned. "Can we trust—?" He turned to the quaking guard. "What's your name?"

"Jerry, Jerry Humbolt. You can trust me."

Able Team pretended to have an argument over whether they could trust the man or not. Pol and Gadgets engaged in a heated exchange while Humbolt tried desperately to hear.

Lyons squatted in front of the frightened guard again. "Well, Jerry, it looks like we're going to give you a chance."

"And the first thing you can do to show your gratitude is to tell me where Allah's Blade does most of its talking," Gadgets said.

Obviously grateful for the chance to get to his feet, the guard jumped up and offered to guide him.

Gadgets placed two of his microminiature bugs where Humbolt could see them. "That's all I need you for,"

Schwarz said as he escorted him back to Lyons, who waited in the lobby. After Humbolt returned to Lyons, Schwarz placed two more under the edge of the carpet.

"Time to get the hell out of here," the Ironman ordered.

"Let's put these AKs back," Gadgets suggested. "They'll wonder why they've been walking around."

"Let's pull back to that building over there," Lyons said, pointing at a small beige structure sitting on a slight knoll. "We can set up in their parking lot. Pol, see if you can get the building manager's permission to park there."

Gadgets returned, grinning. "I put the AKs back, but I pulled their teeth."

10

The three remaining Allah's Blade terrorists and the Horde's five street warriors returned jubilantly from their mission to the *R. P. Zinglow*. Most slapped the guard on the back as they entered the complex.

"Good operation," Razul bragged.

Genghis squinted at Jerry Humbolt and jabbed him in the ribs. "Rock-and-roll time."

With each comment, the uniformed guard nodded and smiled his approval. Humbolt hoped the fear swelling in his chest didn't show. He knew that if he reported the CIA's visit he'd be interrogated.

Ever the tactician, the Horde's chief sent all but Mok out to secure the perimeter. "Make sure we don't get any surprise visitors. Bring me a radio from the car. Stay in contact."

The hit team were exhausted but they were all having trouble settling down. Humbolt made himself invisible by constantly making rounds.

Genghis produced a cardboard box he'd carried in from the car.

"You brought money?" Alonzo Black asked; he was still mentioning his payment at every opportunity.

"My choice of bacteria." Genghis laughed and lifted a bottle of Scotch out with two fingers. "We have less than twenty-four hours to wait, so how about some R and R?"

Colonel Razul nodded. "A celebration is in order. What else do you have in the box?"

"Just the standard all-American goodies. More Scotch and, would you believe, speed and a little hash?"

Alonzo put his hand on the box. "Look here. None of this would have happened without my bugs. I want in on the celebration."

"What'll it be?" asked the big Chinese leader. "Booze or a well-refined chemical substance?"

Petulant because he hadn't received the treatment heroes were due, Alonzo sulked. "Nothing. If I was properly paid, we could really party. What we need is a little entertainment of the female variety." He walked out of the room, muttering to himself.

The Horde's chief turned to Colonel Razul. "You'd better keep him happy until we get his invention under your control."

Incensed at being advised by a street punk, Razul bristled. "What would you suggest, a bottle and a nipple?"

Pulling on his Mongolian mustache, the L.A. gang leader glanced at the colonel. "No, I think you should rent him a woman. That's all he thinks about."

"Find him one."

"Mok," Genghis ordered, "find Patti and Jean and tell them to work the good doctor over."

THREE HOURS LATER, the guard escorted the two tackily dressed women from the complex. Humbolt returned to his task of maintaining a low profile. Every squeak, every little sound, reminded him of his vulnerable position. Fear kept the taste of iron permanently in his mouth.

Tired of watching the portable TV for news of the tanker, Tabina double-checked that the guard had locked the door before joining the big Chinese leader.

"Did you find those two prostitutes attractive?" she asked him without any preamble.

"They were okay."

Inhaling a Ritz cigarette, she hesitated, then blew a cloud of smoke in his face. "Do you find me attractive?" She ran her index finger down the scar on his face.

Without taking his eyes from hers, Genghis took her wrist and pulled the willing terrorist against his chest. "Can you do what they do—better?"

She stared into his eyes. Sliding her hand under his vest, then down his chest, she murmured, "I'm the best. Don't take my word for it. Check." She pulled him toward the lounge.

Colonel Ziyad Razul watched his daughter humiliating the family name, but Allah's Blade needed the help of the Horde so badly that he remained silent. But someday, Genghis, he thought, I'll make you pay for this. Razul's whistle was so low only he could hear it.

REFLECTED LIGHT from a full moon added to the illumination in the telephone booth. It also increased the Ironman's feeling of vulnerability. His midnight report to Stony Man wasn't going well. Brognola already knew everything he had to tell him.

"We know Allah's Blade hit the tanker, Carl," Brognola insisted, switching from the telephone to the bitch box. "Aaron and his computers figured it out."

Hal had to turn the volume down when Lyons yelled, "What the hell do you need us for, then? Just ask the computer." Lyons guessed that Kurtzman was laughing to himself.

Lyons's guess hit the bull's-eye. "Right on, Ironman," the Bear yelled.

Patiently Brognola tried to appease Lyons. "Isn't one of the hookers who visited Allah's Blade named Jean?"

"Yes."

"Didn't she leave before midnight?"

"Yes."

"Well, Ironman, she had another john within an hour of leaving Dnathro."

"Who the hell did she find, Kurtzman?"

Hal chuckled at the look on Aaron's face. "No, Carl, but she might as well have. She turned a trick with a Coast Guard radio operator who just happened to be on duty when the *R. P. Zinglow* massacre surfaced. Evidently, in the heat of passion, your Dr. Black told her about the *Zinglow*, and she repeated it."

"And?" Lyons demanded, getting impatient.

"And he called the duty officer at the station, who called the FBI. Aaron input the data and came up with Allah's Blade."

Lyons closed his eyes, rubbing his puzzled brow, before asking for a report on the ship.

"Entire crew of thirty-two dead, and its cargo in the process of turning into a substance that hardly resembles oil," Hal answered. "The technical people say that within less than twenty-four hours everything in the holds will be affected."

"Colonel Razul and his followers have a lot of paying to do," Lyons declared. He described Able Team's present situation.

"We're trying to keep this tanker problem out of the media," Brognola advised. "It looks like Allah's Blade won't involve Libya until they get confirmation of the effectiveness of the bacteria. We've got to be careful and get the people that Allah's Blade intends to do business with."

Staying in the shadow of the building, Schwarz managed to catch Lyons's attention. "We've got trouble. Looks like a recon on our position—the beepers are indicating that the Horde is moving this way. And they've got radios."

Lyons moved from the public telephone back to the car. "Can you either hear or jam them?"

"Yes, but not both at the same time. Which do you want?"

"Listen," Lyons told him.

"C.C. TO GENGHIS, C.C. to Genghis."

"Genghis here. What's the problem?"

"Looks like company."

"Where?"

"North of us, on a little hill. I think I saw movement near a parked car."

"Could be somebody making out," the Horde's chief reasoned. "Take a look and check in."

"You got it."

Darkness served as an ally to both groups. Able Team, having monitored the transmission, set up a parking scene with Gadgets and Pol in the vehicle. Ironman backed them up from the bushes.

A number of eucalyptus trees decorated the knoll in front of the car. C.C., the Latino and another soldier scurried from shadow to shadow. Stopping as close as cover would allow, the soldier checked in.

"Talk to me," Genghis commanded.

"You may be right. It looks like it's just a little makin' out. Hold it. Hold it. That's two dudes."

"Hassle 'em," ordered the Horde's chief. "If they're for real, mug 'em. If not, waste 'em."

Both Gadgets and Blancanales heard the transmission. They reached for their silenced Berettas and warned Lyons by clicking their radio.

The big Mexican scrambled over to the edge of the building, his AK ready.

"I wonder which one of the Kalashnikovs they're carrying," Gadgets whispered. "Odds are sixty-six percent in our favor they're toting weapons that won't fire."

By now the Latino had crawled to the edge of the parking lot. He rolled over once and sprang to his feet, his rifle pointed at Pol's head. His move was so sudden it surprised both men.

"Hey, man. What happenin'? This is a private lover's lane, man. Like boys and girls. Dig?"

Pol rolled his eyes and winked. "Hey, buddy, what's your prob? We're just good friends. You understand, don't you?" He put his hand on Gadgets's knee.

Signaling over the top of the car with his left hand, the Latino motioned for one of the other soldiers to move in.

The muscular Mexican slipped up and opened the door. "What have we here? A couple of *mariposas*?" He cocked his head and winked.

"What the hell's a *mariposa*?" demanded the black soldier.

Flapping his arms like a bird, the Mexican grinned. "A butterfly, man, a fucking butterfly."

"Well, butterfly or whatever, let's have your wallets. Now." All the light banter disappeared, and street-hardened eyes focused on the intended victims.

Ironman had picked up the change in conversational tone and moved in behind the Latino. He placed the cold end of his Python against the spot where the spine meets the skull.

"Unless you want to make this your last job, you'd better—"

Before he could finish his statement, Lyons felt the tip of a knife blade press into the same spot on the back of his neck.

"No, man. Unless *you* want to have your brains served up as breakfast, you'd better drop that cannon." C.C.'s eyes were sparkling.

"Careful," Lyons cautioned, using the agreed-upon code word.

Everything happened at once.

Lyons pivoted forward and to his right in a spinning backfist move with his .357 magnum.

Blancanales fired his 93-R from under his arm as Gadgets pulled the trigger of his Beretta.

The slug from Pol's shot entered the black soldier just beneath his chin, tore up through his mouth and finally shattered his skull. He hadn't even had time to raise his weapon.

Schwarz's parabellum hornet stung the Latino in the throat, buzzing through to his spine. His eyes shone with the love of combat—to live or to die—as he fell over backward, trying to pull the trigger on a weapon with a defective firing pin.

But Ironman swung into trouble. As he moved into his spinning backfist, his Mongolian attacker stepped back and raised his razor-sharp bowie knife. The sharp edge came down toward Lyons's swinging arm. The Stony Man warrior knew that if he continued his move he risked losing his hand.

C.C. grinned. "Come and get it, mutha."

Three rapid-fire rounds coughed from Pol's silenced 93-R.

The Mongolian's right elbow shattered, and the knife expert screamed, "Pig!"

Continuing his pivot, Lyons fired his Python just as the sights crossed C.C.'s chest.

The slender killer lurched backward, trying to follow the slug as it vacated his body. His right hand still gripped the useless bowie.

Ironman felt a tickling sensation down his back. He reached around to scratch, but instinctively he knew that the itch was caused by a trickle of blood.

"That's as close as I ever want to get to the end of a bowie," he said as Pol applied enough pressure on the neck wound to stop the bleeding.

"I'm surprised," Schwarz confessed.

The two other members of Able Team looked at him.

He shrugged. "I thought Ironman's neck would at least dull a little ol' bowie knife. Guess not."

"We don't have time to play nurse," Lyons griped, pulling away from Pol. "They heard that shot down there, and we better cover them quick. Check these AKs and see if the one you didn't screw up is here."

"One Kalashnikov was good and the other bad," reported Gadgets.

"That means the remaining one won't fire. Good. Let's use the car to check out Dnathro," Lyons ordered, jumping into the back seat.

11

The sounds of battle echoed through the empty halls of Dnathro. The Horde's leader clicked his radio.

"C.C., C.C. C'mon."

Genghis repeated his call three times, waited and tried again. Nothing.

"We got a problem. Mok, take a look. Don't mix it up. See who's on our ass." He turned toward the colonel. "We'd better split."

Genghis snapped his fingers at Akmet, taking control of the situation. "Get the bacteria and the doctor up here. Tabina, take the last rifle. Cover our rear."

Outside, Mok watched Able Team's car start and head toward Dnathro. He ran on an intercept course and hid in a patch of philodendrons growing near the Pipette Street entrance. Sighting over his Colt Peacemaker, the Horde's warlord grinned as he recalled being warned that his hands were too small to handle the weapon. He aimed dead center on the grill, knowing that his FJ slugs would tear through the radiator and most of the way through the engine. He fired and rolled.

The flash connected, and the car's engine froze, a twisted piece of scrap. Mok watched as Able Team bailed out, the men running in different directions.

The warlord ran to his right, away from the street.

The shot was heard inside Dnathro. "Only one," Genghis announced. "Had to be Mok. If they were attacking they'd be laying down some lead. Get ready to bust out of here."

Again Razul followed his orders.

Without anyone having noticed his entry, the Horde's warlord was standing beside Genghis.

"Roberto and Cuts Clean—wasted."

A slight movement in the muscles in the big Chinese leader's jaw indicated that he'd heard. A shudder rippled across his back. Genghis rubbed the center of his forehead with the middle fingers of his right hand.

Needing to break the silence, Mok continued, "Took out their car. There's only three of 'em. This'll grab you, boss. One of them looked like that guy that hassled you in La Jolla."

Genghis shifted his feet like a batter getting ready for a pitch. He pressed his palms together in the Buddhist fashion, placing the tips of his fingers against his mouth. "They were good men. Mok, you and I are going to avenge our brothers. Carl Lyons is going to die. Let's move out."

"What about the guard?" Tabina asked, deeply inhaling her Ritz cigarette.

"Kill him," Genghis said. "We don't need to leave a squawk box behind for the FBI or the CIA to interrogate."

Colonel Ziyad Razul finally realized he'd given up command of the operation to a street punk. "Hold it. I'm in charge here. I'll decide who does what." He slapped his leg with his swagger stick.

Genghis whirled. "Are you more interested in playing king of the hill or in showing our enemy that we are a force to be reckoned with? Everyone knows you're in charge."

Mok put his hand on his gun and stepped away from the wall. With a slight intake of breath, Tabina reached for her purse and a 9 mm Browning. Akmet went for his AK-47, while Alonzo Black cowered against the wall.

Before Razul could reply, the guard returned from completing his rounds on the second floor. "Did you hear that shot?" he asked breathlessly.

Colonel Razul, choosing to ignore Genghis, turned toward Humbolt and motioned for the guard to come over.

Suspicious because of the unnatural silence in the room, Humbolt hesitated. His eyes darted from face to face. Sweat beads glistened on his forehead.

Angry at his defiance, Razul pointed at the floor in front of his feet. "Now."

Intimidated, the security officer responded. "Sure, boss." His eyes kept checking the others. Everyone wore very bland expressions.

Razul stuck his hand out. "We're leaving. Thank your people for the assistance. This building and your service to our cause were invaluable."

Caught off guard by the colonel's friendliness, Humbolt reached for his hand. "Glad to be able to—"

The words froze in his throat. Humbolt's jaws moved like those of a hooked bass. No sound escaped. He collapsed to the floor, fighting for air.

Genghis tugged on his mustache. Before he could respond to Razul's demonstration, Tabina's portable TV broadcast a news flash.

"Silence," the leader of Allah's Blade commanded. "This could be it."

The shot of the anchor of the twenty-four-hour news program faded to a scene on the deck of a supertanker. The cameraman scanned the ship's name on the bridge, then moved down the deck to show a double row of body bags, before framing the reporter.

"A spokesman for the Coast Guard reports they have never encountered such brutal slayings," she began.

There was another shot of the body bags and then a scan of the blood-spattered walls of the crew quarters.

"It appears that the ship's entire cargo of crude oil has been destroyed. Chemists are now..." The screen went blank; then the anchorman returned.

"Ladies and gentlemen, we seem to be having transmission difficulties. When the problem is resolved, we'll continue our coverage of this story."

Alonzo Black's face lit up like a kid's on Christmas morning. "I delivered what I promised, now where's my money? I want to celebrate."

Colonel Razul moved a step closer to Alonzo. "Until we can duplicate your process, you stay with us," he stated in a soft voice.

Stunned, the scientist blinked; then he laughed. "I have the complete recipe in a safety-deposit box. When I get paid, you'll have it. Duplicating it is easy, but keeping it alive until you feed it oil is impossible—without my formula."

"You will stay with us until we know how it works," explained the commander.

Agitated by the conversation and still boiling over the loss of his men, Genghis wanted action. "Let's get out of here. Where are we headed?"

Razul hesitated before answering. "Santa Barbara for a meeting with the Brotherhood."

"And if we get separated? Where will I contact you?"

Again Razul hesitated. "Our meet is set for two days from now, Santa Barbara. Six o'clock in front of a statue of three dolphins."

"Six o'clock. I'll be there," Genghis promised. "I will recruit additional manpower on my way there."

Razul saluted with his swagger stick. "Shall we liberate some Libyan oil money?"

12

His left thumb stuck under his bandolier, General Mousa paced, stopped and stared at Colonel Konstantin. "Is your team ready?"

Konstantin pursed his lips, nodding. "Yes. More than ready. They're anxiously awaiting the opportunity to serve the motherland."

"How do you intend to ensure that we acquire this formula?"

"We have activated a Spetsnaz group out of Canada." The colonel's eyes remained a flat black. The blade of his pocketknife scraped nonexistent dirt from under his right thumbnail. He knew that he had to falsely assure his superior.

"Good. Allah's blessing be on their endeavor," answered General Mousa. He wished for only one thing: death to the Americans and their advanced technology. Those who raped the holy Berber territories with endless crews of oil workers would witness the rapid destruction of their work. How one arrived at that victory was irrelevant, but hanging the enemy with his own rope would be a bonus. A rope developed by an American—the irony satisfied his Arab soul. Beautiful. And Konstantin represented an adequate pawn in the game.

"Let's dine," he suggested. "A precelebration is in order for your friends from the north." The general hoped the alcohol served with dinner would loosen the Russian's tongue.

"To *Rodina*," the colonel finally slurred. Staggering to his feet, he mumbled, "I must leave. Tomorrow I select the backup strike team."

Before he could turn to make his way to the door, Konstantin passed out, falling across the table. General Mousa had the drunk Russian delivered to the ship where the frogmen would be chosen.

COLONEL MARKUS KONSTANTIN lay motionless on his bunk. Just attempting to open his eyes increased the pain. Vodka pain. Finally he pried one eye open, realized the time and stumbled for the head. "That fucking Mousa almost destroyed me." Cold water brought with it the realization that he was aboard a ship. Shaking his head, he mentally congratulated the general on his ploy. Somehow the Arab had discovered he had to witness the selection of the strike team. He shuddered in the cold water, then dressed quickly and made his way out onto the deck.

One hundred and fifty volunteer frogmen of the Soviet Naval Infantry waited patiently in line to be interviewed for a mission that was rumored to be of great importance. Scuttlebutt had it that a hero's medal would be awarded—to anyone who survived.

It took four hours to settle on the commander, Captain Stefan Popov, an experienced army veteran. The fifteen additional men took another six hours.

"Comrades, your talents are superior to those of your comrades. I salute you. *Nazdarovye!*"

In return, the men lifted their glasses in unison. *"Nazdarovye!"*

Comrade Colonel Markus Konstantin welcomed the healing burn of the vodka.

13

The evening was a Santa Barbara beauty. Oranges and yellows flashed, reflecting off the water and painting the scattered wisps of clouds.

Seated on the balcony of the Sea Star Motel, his heels resting on the railing, Comrade Major Omar Khalid looked over the toes of his polished boots toward an offshore derrick. The continuous *click-click* of his grip-strengthening device accented the traffic noise.

The gym had been full of undedicated people, he mused, but the equipment had impressed him. A two-hour workout was as much as anyone on undercover duty could work in. He frowned. He'd already lost the pumped feeling he enjoyed so much. He needed another session.

Khalid knew that even a good workout would fail to lift his depression. Though he had been chosen as leader of the Libyans, he knew that whatever he accomplished would be credited to Tariq Akmet, General Mousa's right-hand man.

"Akmet tells me the Horde has already lost three men. When did he say Allah's Blade will arrive?" Lieutenant Fessi asked, pulling his left arm against his side for the hundredth time to ensure that he still carried his .45 ACP.

"You mean *Major* Akmet," Khalid snapped, still smarting over Akmet's obviously preferred position with the general. He squeezed the spring-connected handles at a faster pace. "They are supposed to be here by six o'clock tomorrow night, according to our contact's report." Khalid refused to say Akmet's name again.

"Do you think that bacteria he called about is really as good as he reported?"

"General Mousa thinks so, and the newscast from last night confirms it. Our small test produced the same results. But it's hard to believe that Colonel Razul was clever enough to come up with such a find. He's tough, but not very smart," Khalid answered, pointing at his head with the hand-squeezer.

"What about the gang of street punks he's hired to back him up?" Fessi asked.

"The Horde. That's what they call themselves."

"Do they present a problem?"

Khalid laughed. "Only when we're through with them. They work for us."

Fessi jumped to his feet and put his back to the railing so that he could look into the major's eyes. "They work for us?"

"Until we have all we need. Then they'll join Allah's Blade at the bottom of the ocean," Khalid bragged. He gripped the handles as hard as possible; then he released one handle, snapping it like a trigger. "But we do have two problems."

The lieutenant waited for his volatile commander to continue.

"First, our contact man inside Allah's Blade lost two of his men on the way to his first meet. The Horde also lost three men to some strike team."

Fessi broke out in a cold sweat. "FBI?"

Khalid shrugged. "It could be that some federal organization is after Allah's Blade—or the Russians, or the Chinese—or even the Israelis. Who knows? All prizes have many competitors. We just have to strike hard and move out fast."

"Where will we have the test?"

"See that drilling platform?" He pointed with his toe. "We'll use an oil barge that's tied up alongside."

"What about their crews?"

"They'll create the identical headlines as the *R. P. Zinglow*. We have a jet standing by. Fifteen minutes after we have the formula it will be on its way home. Then Libya will be able to reduce the available oil supply."

"And—" Fessi laughed "—raise our prices to a decent level." Rising with a salute, he said, "Excuse me, comrade major, I must tell the rest of the men."

Khalid's eyes narrowed. "Idiot. We are officers and we should know all, but they are soldiers. The less they know, the better. Sit—and stop saluting."

ABLE TEAM, knowing that Allah's Blade planned to link up with the Brotherhood thanks to Gadgets's well-placed bugs, went on ahead. Gadgets and Pol paired up, and Lyons rented another car.

"There's only one major highway to Santa Barbara from the south," the Ironman informed his partners. "You two wait for that bugged AK to show up in either the yellow Mercedes or the black Cad and I'll see what can be done to find the Libyan terrorists. Now, I think I'd better check in with Stony Man."

"Good work on uncovering the Blade's next move," Brognola congratulated him. "We have data on the involvement of General Mousa and his comrades. The

Brotherhood commander you're looking for is a Major Omar Khalid. He's Mousa's right hand.''

"Know anything about him?''

"A little. He's originally from a small Berber tribe in North Africa, educated in England. He hates Americans. He also refuses to admit he's a Berber.''

"Figures. Anything else?''

"Yes. He's loaded. Made it in oil when the price peaked. He's also a health nut. Works out four, five hours a day on weights and karate.'' Brognola chuckled. "Just like you, except for the money.''

"*F-u-n-n-y,*'' the Ironman spelled.

"Congratulations on your spelling,'' Brognola teased. "You're a scholar and a weight lifter.''

Lyons ignored the banter. Only Omar Khalid interested him.

Kurtzman broke in. "I have the rest of his physical description as listed in the CIA files.''

Ironman shook his head and smiled as Aaron read the contents of the limited-access file.

"Anything else I might identify him by?''

"He wears a big diamond pinkie ring. Never takes it off,'' Brognola inserted.

"Anything else?''

"Only this. The President has put Allah's Blade, the Horde and the Brotherhood in our lap.''

"Does this mean a clean sweep?''

"You know we can't officially order a hit, but if they should threaten you or get in the way...'' Brognola shrugged. "Those things happen.''

"Gotcha.''

"Ironman?''

"Yes?''

"The President wants that bacteria—all of it.''

"You got it."

Before he left the booth, Ironman looked up all the gyms in Santa Barbara. Three. He decided to start with the one nearest the beach. He could use a workout anyway.

THE MISSING MIXTURE of sweat, Ben-Gay, grungy workout clothes and shouted obscenities told the Able Team warrior he'd found one of those gyms that replaced singles bars. Color-coordinated sweats and little honeys hustling everything but weights filled the Fitness Haven.

Two private phone booths and matching tiled walls replaced the standard cracked mirrors, cloud of graffiti and battered wall phone.

"Disgusting," Lyons muttered.

Instead of the ever-present hustler draped over the phone trying to explain to his old lady why he'd spent the rent money on health food and beer, sweeties giggled with pencil-necked yuppies about the latest flavor of yogurt.

Ironman went into the locker room to change. It shone enough to make a serious lifter cry. Neat. No broken lockers with discarded sweats hanging on the doors, no lost Adidas lying in the corner, and not so much as half a bar of soap on the floor.

Lyons's entrance into the gym was just that, an entrance. Not accustomed to seeing serious weight lifters, everyone acknowledged him by staring. He walked to the back of the large room. A squat rack and pressing bench sat unused. A good set of Olympic weights and graduated dumbbells were all Lyons needed for a private workout.

After warming up, Ironman cinched his lifting belt tight. He chuckled to himself as he noted that he was the only one in the gym with a sweat-stained tank top. He warmed up with a set of light squats. Evidently his idea of light turned out to be a bit more than the others had seen. One by one, people hesitated between exercises to watch him. When he loaded up to do some serious lifting, the conversation level dropped.

Following his first set, a slender young man approached. He stuck his hand out. "I'm the owner. We normally don't get you big guys here. It's surprising. You're the second lifter we've had today."

"Oh? Why do you suppose that is?"

"We don't cater to your, er, type."

Lyons slipped under the bar for the next set. "And what type am I?"

The manager was warming to the sound of his own voice, and he couldn't wait to expound his theories.

"Conservative, right-winger. Pro-death penalty, pro-military, pro-police, pro-counterstrike and against anything the communists do."

"Sounds pretty positive."

"The other side is positive, too."

"Tell me."

"Sure. Pro-abortion, pro-criminal's rights, pro-communist, pro-government control."

"And you've decided that the second group make better customers?"

"Sure do. I can sell them anything as long as it's in. They'd eat burnt lizard skins for breakfast if the liberals said President Reagan hated them."

Ironman worked through his second set. More members stopped to admire the show of strength.

"And where do you stand?" Lyons asked.

"Somewhere to the right of Attila the Hun, but—" he shrugged "—business is business."

Ironman bent over to catch his breath. He had just one set to go before finishing his squats. Suddenly a dark-skinned Middle Eastern lifter in shorts and a tank top stalked over to the lifting platform. Welcome, Major Khalid, the Able Team commando thought. Without a word, Khalid began unloading the squat bar.

"Hold it, friend. I've only got one more set and you can have it," Lyons said.

The stranger ignored him and continued removing the forty-five-pound plates.

Lyons straightened, picked up two plates and slid one back on the opposite end. He walked around to the other side. "I'm not through." He pushed himself between Khalid and the other end. "Excuse me."

By now others had noticed the action and stopped to watch.

A red flush started at his chest and radiated upward from the terrorist's tank top. "I would suggest you stop trying to interfere with my workout," the Berber threatened.

Lyons stabbed his index finger into the air between his eyes. "Look, I told you I only had one more set. If you don't understand American manners, go back to your tent and play in the sand."

The gym exploded with laughter.

Khalid cursed. He was still holding on to his last plate, and it was obvious that his control was slipping. Seeing Lyons casually walk over to the center of the rack and set his feet pushed the man over the edge.

Ironman, balanced for a sudden move, watched Major Khalid struggle with his temper.

"Imperialist pig," the Berber screamed. He attempted to throw the plate. It clattered to the platform, and Lyons sidestepped it.

"Easy with that Frisbee, you'll hurt yourself." Lyons assumed the horse position, setting himself for the charge he knew would follow the plate.

Khalid charged the laughing Carl Lyons. A vertical leap into the same side thrust kick snapped out.

With the ease of a fifth-degree karate instructor teaching a white belt, Lyons stepped sideways and blocked Khalid's extended leg with an outside forearm blow. Instead of countering, he shifted to an aikido stance.

Still loaded for combat, the terrorist bounded to his feet. He shot a round kick at Lyons's head.

With a grin for the benefit of his audience, the Ironman stepped back half an inch and grasped Khalid's leg. At the peak of the Berber's motion, the Ironman tightened his grip on his ankle. He pivoted, utilizing all the terrorist's force, and upended the charging Arab. The back of the surprised attacker's head struck the platform, knocking him into a dull, gray cloud of unconsciousness.

Lyons picked him up and laid him on a pressing bench. "I'll finish my set now." He replaced the missing plates and grunted through his last group of squats.

Major Omar Khalid, who had considered himself indestructible, lay as still as a six-year-old napping during a kindergarten rest period.

The Able Team warrior walked around the prone terrorist, straddled the bench behind Omar's head and lifted his body to a sitting position. He placed the tips of his index fingers in the depression behind a clavicle, stabbing down and toward the center of Khalid's heart.

A shock wave exploded through the Arab's body, blasting him awake. Khalid's head snapped upright at the same time his eyes opened.

"Oooooofff!" An elbow slammed into the Ironman's ribs.

Khalid bounded off the bench, shooting a rear thrust kick at Lyons's head. "A present for you, musclehead."

By moving a fraction of an inch, Lyons avoided the kick. "School time." He flattened himself on the bench, beating the follow-up kick.

Again the working end of the gym had become a stage. The crowd formed a semicircle around the combatants, cheering for the Arab.

Tired of the bullshit, Ironman didn't bother to leave the bench. Following Khalid's last back kick, Lyons shot a lightning-fast heel kick into the terrorist's groin. The Arab tried dodging the rapierlike thrust but was unsuccessful. A bolt of pain closed Khalid's mind to thoughts of revenge, fighting, showing off and breathing. He collapsed on the floor.

Lyons glanced toward the manager to see if there would be any flak.

A smile, a wink and a sly thumbs-up answered his unspoken question.

Before the Libyan could recover his bearings, Lyons slipped out. Positioning himself across the street, he waited to follow the terrorist to his command center.

Within five minutes the deflated terrorist left the gymnasium. He walked toward the ocean. His gait slowly increased until he was jogging. Khalid shook his head as he ran. Soon he was running in bursts, jogging for a block and then dashing for a block. By the time he reached the Sea Star Motel, his swagger had returned.

Lyons had followed in his car. When Khalid went into the motel, Ironman called the rest of the Team on their secure-frequency NSA hand radio.

"Ironman calling Blancanales and Schwarz. Ironman calling Blancanales and Schwarz. C'mon."

"Terrible twins here. Gadgets speaking. How goes it?"

"Good. I've located our target."

"Nothing here yet. We found a motel with a view of both the north and south lanes of Highway 5. Any change of plans?" asked Schwarz.

"I'd like one of your bugs to attach itself to the target. What motel and what room?"

"We're at the Hacienda, right at the entrance to Santa Barbara, room 221, Talamantez and Klein."

"I'll be by for you in ten minutes. Lyons out."

"After locating the Hacienda, Lyons asked Pol to call the Sea Star to determine Khalid's room number.

After only a short conversation, Pol turned to Ironman. "Our target is located in room 202. He has a double with one other person."

"There's got to be more soldiers than that," Lyons muttered. "That's too few for the kind of operation they have in mind."

Schwarz grinned. "My little friends might be able to help."

"Leave me a direction finder. I'll stay here and listen for Allah's Blade. You and Pol see if you can penetrate Khalid's room. Bug it."

"Consider it done," Gadgets told him.

14

Carl Lyons settled back for a long, boring wait. To make his job a bit more interesting, he moved out to the balcony. At least he could see more there, although he really didn't need to if the direction finder functioned. It would sing out with loud beeps if Razul's Mercedes approached.

During the first hour he reviewed everything he could remember about Allah's Blade. Then, using his watch to check, he practiced count-timing. Usually he could estimate ten-, fifteen- and thirty-second periods accurately, but when he moved up to a full minute he always rushed it by two seconds. He kept practicing. Sometimes he used his pulse, and sometimes just a slow count. Lyons knew that relying on his pulse rate for timing in a tense situation was dangerous. Adrenaline accelerated the clock.

Ironman hated waiting. He was a man of action—action meant he wasn't letting life pass him by. And it was the filler that kept painful memories from resurfacing.

"Commitment. The story of my life," Lyons said to a sparrow cocking its head as it searched the balcony for food. "You committed to anything?" he asked the bird. "Probably not. You're just like much of the rest of the world. Belly first."

The saucy sparrow continued its search. Its tenacity reminded Lyons of a dog he'd kept as a pet when he was ten.

Caesar had looked as though he'd been assembled from a box of spare parts. An oversize brown-and-black Scottie's head had topped a black Airedale body supported by a greyhound's long tan legs. A bright pair of light brown eyes had challenged all those who came into contact with him. He'd started out as a rambunctious puppy whose loyalty went to anyone who would throw him a ball. But quickly he'd become ten-year-old Carl Lyons's best friend.

When Caesar was still a puppy, Carl took him to the veterinarian for his distemper shots. Frightened by the strange smells, Caesar shook like a Watusi warrior in an igloo.

"C'mon, Caesar. I'm right here. This won't hurt you very much. It's for your own good." The boy insisted his dog didn't need muzzling, but the vet tied off his mouth anyway.

Rolling his eyes helplessly at his young master, Caesar tried wagging his tail.

By now, Lyons's eyes were tear-rimmed and red, and he had to blink to keep them open. As the doctor advanced with the needle, the boy promised his best friend he'd never let anyone hurt him.

The crazy mixed-up mutt took his shot without flinching. Lyons hadn't, but he renewed his promise to protect his friend—no matter what. Even then, Lyons honored his vows.

At the age of twelve he discovered the cost of that personality trait.

On weekends he took Caesar to an undeveloped hilly area and released him. Lyons would sit by the hour watching his buddy pirouette through the brush of the Los Angeles hills, chasing anything that moved. Periodically the dog returned to his master's side to rest. During these periods the boy shared all his deepest secrets. Caesar understood every problem.

For almost two years they spent at least one day a week on the hills. Until an airhead fanatic looking for action for his pit bulls discovered the spot. Along with his vanload of battle-hardened pits, he brought a buddy and a camper filled with neighborhood dogs he'd stolen to use as sparring partners.

Caesar stopped chasing rabbits and stood stock-still, barking furiously. He wouldn't respond to the boy's call or whistle. Frustrated by his dog's refusal to return, Lyons set out to find him.

"C'mon, Caesar," the young boy yelled. The dog increased his racket.

By the time Lyons reached his dog, his temper had reached the boiling point. "Damn you, Caesar, who do you think you are?" He topped a knoll with three manzanita bushes clustered near the summit. Caesar stopped barking and started howling.

"I called you at least ten times and I expect—" Lyons blinked, shook his head and stumbled over to his dog. Scattered in heaps were the mutilated remains of at least a dozen dogs. Poodles, a bulldog, a couple of cockers and the torn fur and bloody carcasses of animals that were now unidentifiable.

Caesar ran behind Carl and pushed him toward the carnage with his head.

Keeping his lunch down proved impossible. After looking over the remains, the boy retrieved the victims' collars and raced his dog home.

It made the news. Big. His mother even appeared on a talk show with someone from the Humane Society. But talk proved to be all that happened. No one was arrested. For two weeks Lyons and Caesar basked in the limelight. But as all tragedies, time heals the greatest outrages. Everyone forgot the event, and the pair headed back to their special playground.

A month later the same vehicles arrived with a load of sparring partners and their warriors-in-training—seven pit bulls.

A man wearing a pair of dirty mechanic's coveralls whined to the driver of the van, "Shit, Dan, why do you want to come back here? They might be lookin' for us."

"Forget 'em. I go where I want, when I want."

"B-but Dan," stammered Festus, "I sure don't want to go to jail. This last batch I got here is from Beverly Hills. They'll cut my balls off if they catch me." As he complained, he snapped a lead onto a Kerry blue terrier.

A low growl starting deep in the brindle Staffordshire terrier's throat startled the Kerry blue. He strained against the rope, trying to reach the pit.

"Hold that mutt," Dan ordered. He jerked the pit's leash. "Major, you want that little shit over there?" he asked the straining dog. "Do you? Well, Major, maybe you could use a little confidence booster. I'll give him to you if you promise to kill him with a little class."

At the same time, Festus agitated the Kerry. The blue either had guts or didn't know what was in store for him. He barked, then settled into a matching growl as he strained against his leash.

The muscles of Major's shoulders bunched as he lowered himself closer to the ground. His fighting style had evolved into a badgerlike attack in which he came in under his opponent's throat. His newest battle scars glistened in the morning sun.

Both men held the snaps on their dog's collars. "Showtime." Dan nodded, releasing Major at the same instant Festus unhooked his victim.

The Kerry blue bounded toward Major.

"Stay low," Dan yelled. "Low."

With a snarl that sent shivers down Dan's spine, Major went to work. The blue came in high, as all amateurs do. A flash of the pit bull filled his vision. For a moment. Then he knew only extreme pain in his throat, a whirling, a snap and blackness.

His muzzle buried in his opponent's throat, Major stood, his four feet braced, and shook the Kerry blue's corpse like a ragged welcome mat.

"Yes! He came in like a tornado." Dan cheered. "His form is back. Back, do you hear?" He pounded Festus on the back.

Right in the middle of their celebration, a black-and-tan blur streaked past them to land on the killer.

Without even a growl, the attacker clamped his teeth on the back of the pit's neck and jerked both Major and his victim into the air.

"What the fuck—" Dan blurted, trying to process what he had witnessed.

Major released the dead blue and twisted in his attacker's grip.

"Caesar!" The call echoed from about twenty-five yards away. "Caesar!"

"It's that kid we saw on TV," Festus exclaimed.

"Gettin'-even time is here." Dan laughed. "Let's add Colonel to the party." He opened the side door of the van and grabbed a black pit's collar. "C'mon, Colonel, the Major wants you to share in the fun."

Already fired up by the sounds of combat, the black package of muscle and fangs bounded toward his teammate.

Carl Lyons's voice grew closer. The boy was running as he'd never run before. Only muffled growls carried to him. Tears blurred his vision as he imagined Caesar being torn to shreds by the pit bulls. He scanned every inch of the ground near his path, looking for a weapon to help his friend with. He tripped and fell, skinning his face, but leaped back up to continue his rescue.

The pits had a battle on their hands. Though Caesar was too long-legged to tangle with the compact fighting machines, he held his own—until Major and Colonel attacked from opposite sides. He feinted at Major, leaped over his back and got a mouthful of the Colonel's throat. Three shakes and a sudden closing of his jaws left the Colonel out of the fighting army. But even as the black warrior died, Major, coming in low, hit Caesar in the throat.

"Colonel!" Dan yelled. "That street mutt killed Colonel." He turned to the van just as the exhausted boy arrived. "Festus, hold that kid." Dan opened the van and, one by one, released three more fighting machines. "That'll hold you, you fuckin' mongrel."

The man wearing the mechanic's overalls dropped the electric cattle prod he was carrying and tackled Lyons.

Twisting, jerking and biting as hard as he could, Caesar fought his way out of Major's grasp, not by overcoming the pit's immense jaw strength but by leaving neck muscle in the pit's mouth.

"Caesar!" Lyons screamed as blood streamed over his dog's shoulders and chest.

Just then the reinforcements arrived. Three charging weapons of teeth and rage hit Caesar at the same time.

One grasped his right front leg, snapping the bone as if it were a piece of balsa wood.

The sound imprinted itself on the boy's psyche forever. Carl Lyons wept, fought, bit, kicked, butted, elbowed and screamed his way out of Festus's arms.

Fighting on three legs, Caesar had two pits on his neck, one on his leg and one going for his throat. The loss of blood had started to weaken Caesar. But when he saw his master, a renewed surge of energy coursed through him. He shook off the warrior hanging from his neck and caught him in the throat before he hit the ground.

One more of the pits joined Colonel. Caesar staggered, his eyes glazed.

The boy reached the fray. Sobbing his friend's name, he grabbed the nearest pit by the head and tried to pull him off. Unable to budge the dog, he tried kicking. Still helpless, the blood-spattered boy decided to go for their eyes.

"Stop that fuckin' kid. He's blinding my dogs," Dan screamed, running toward him.

Dan grabbed him by the shirttail, trying to pull him away. "Get the fuck away from my dog."

Carl Lyons slipped out of his shirt, running toward Caesar. "I'm coming." He threw his skinny body between his friend and the last killer. His hands fumbled for the dog's throat or eyes. Then darkness captured Lyons as Dan clubbed him across the back of the head with a jack handle.

Hours later, throbbing pain broke into Carl Lyons's consciousness. His first thought: *Caesar*.

First he whispered the dog's name. "Caesar, c'mon, boy. It's all right. I'm here."

Only the distant sounds of L.A. traffic broke the silence.

With the strength that only love can bring, Lyons pushed aside the awareness of his aching head. His concussion limited his sight to tunnel vision. He staggered and fell across the Kerry blue's body. The cold congealed blood stuck to his face. He brushed at it with the back of his hand.

"Caesar."

Darkness threatened to overcome the West Coast sunset. The boy concentrated. He had to find his buddy. Slowly his peripheral vision returned, and he scanned the carnage. The slaughtered Kerry lay next to Colonel. Between two mangled pits lay Caesar. His throat was torn out, and his lips were curled back in a perpetual smile. It was almost as if he were saying, "We gave 'em hell, Carl, real hell."

The boy collapsed to his knees and crawled over to his dead friend.

Hot tears melted the congealed blood on Lyons's cheeks. He gently picked up the big dog's head and held it in his lap. Sobbing, he petted Caesar, telling him that he was the bravest dog in the world. Night fell, and he remained, holding his friend.

"Over here! He's over here."

A spotlight fell on Lyons and Caesar. Still resting the dog's head in his lap, the boy refused to release his friend until Lyons's father promised him a policeman would take the dog to his house.

Ironman swallowed as he remembered his emotions at the death of his best friend. Following that sensation came a flood of satisfaction as he remembered that the judge had sentenced Caesar's murderers to jail.

"Now," he said to the perky sparrow on the balcony railing, "that dog understood commitment."

15

The hot rays of the afternoon sun only added to the Ironman's discomfort. Recalling the loss of Caesar always put him into a depression. He decided to go inside, knowing that the beeper would work there, as well. Maybe a little distraction, like the TV, would get his mind off the bad memories, he thought. He lay back on the bed.

Someone knocked on the door. Lyons's Python filled his fist.

"Yes? Who is it?" He slipped behind the door. When the knob rotated about a sixteenth of an inch, he undid the lock and jerked the door open.

A woman's gray tweed business suit, beautifully rounded out by a startled brunette, flew into the room. She struggled to recover her balance.

Lyons's .357 Magnum centered on her chest.

"Hi, grouch."

"Sherry? What the hell are you doing here?" The Ironman's Python dropped to his side.

"I live here, remember?" Slowly her well-manicured hands smoothed her skirt down over her shapely hips. The skirt ended three inches above her knees.

"Yes, but how did you find me at the Hacienda?"

"I work in a law office. In that white building, second floor," she said, pointing across the freeway.

REWARD! Free Books! Free Gifts!

LUCKY PLAY GOLD EAGLE'S
CARNIVAL WHEEL
SCRATCH-OFF GAME

SCRATCH OFF HERE

FIND OUT **INSTANTLY** IF YOU CAN GET
FREE BOOKS AND A SURPRISE GIFT!

PLAY THE
LUCKY CARNIVAL WHEEL

scratch-off game
and get as many as
FIVE FREE GIFTS...

HOW TO PLAY:

1. With a coin, carefully scratch off the silver area at right. Then check your number against the chart below to see which gifts you can get. If you're lucky, you'll instantly be entitled to receive one or more books and possibly another gift, ABSOLUTELY FREE!

2. Send back this card and we'll promptly send you any Free Gifts you're entitled to. You may get brand-new, red-hot Gold Eagle books and a terrific Surprise Mystery Gift!

3. We're betting you'll want more of these action-packed stories, so we'll send you six more high-voltage books every other month to preview. Always delivered right to your home before they're available in stores. And always at a hefty saving off the retail price!

4. Your satisfaction is guaranteed! You may return any shipment of books and cancel any time. The Free Books and Gift remain yours to keep!

NO COST! NO RISK!
NO OBLIGATION TO BUY!

FREE SURPRISE MYSTERY GIFT!

We can't tell you what it is—that would spoil the surprise—but it could be yours FREE when you play the **"LUCKY CARNIVAL WHEEL"** scratch-off game!

PLAY THE LUCKY
"CARNIVAL WHEEL"

Just scratch off the silver area above with a coin. Then look for your number on the chart below to see which gifts you can get!

YES! I have scratched off the silver box. Please send me all the gifts I'm entitled to receive. I understand that I am under no obligation to purchase any more books. I may keep these free gifts and return my statement marked "cancel." If I do not cancel, then send me 6 brand-new Gold Eagle novels every second month as they come off the presses. Bill me at the low price of $2.49 for each book—a saving of 11% off the total retail price for six books—plus 95¢ postage and handling per shipment. I can always return a shipment and cancel at any time. The Free Books and Surprise Mystery Gift remain mine to keep forever.

166 CIM PAPB

NAME_____
(Please Print)

ADDRESS_____APT. NO._____

CITY_____STATE_____ZIP CODE_____

39	WORTH FOUR FREE BOOKS AND A FREE SURPRISE GIFT
30	WORTH FOUR FREE BOOKS
5	WORTH THREE FREE BOOKS
16	WORTH TWO FREE BOOKS AND A FREE SURPRISE GIFT

Offer limited to one per household and not valid for present subscribers. Terms and prices subject to change.

CLAIM YOUR FREE GIFTS! MAIL THIS CARD TODAY!

Guns, Guts and Glory!

America's most potent human weapons take on the world's barbarians! Meet them—join them—in a war of vengeance against terrorists, anarchists, hijackers and drug dealers! Mack Bolan and his courageous squads, Able Team & Phoenix Force—along with SOBs and Vietnam: Ground Zero unleash the best sharpshooting firepower ever published!

If offer card is missing, write to: Gold Eagle Reader Service, 901 Fuhrmann Blvd., P.O. Box 1394, Buffalo, NY 14269-1394

► MAIL THIS CARD TODAY! ◄

BUSINESS REPLY CARD

First Class   Permit No. 717   Buffalo, NY

Postage will be paid by addressee

Gold Eagle Reader Service
901 Fuhrmann Blvd.
P.O. Box 1394
Buffalo, NY 14240-9963

NO POSTAGE
NECESSARY
IF MAILED
IN THE
UNITED STATES

"How did you recognize me?"

"By your scars."

Carl frowned. He knew she was putting him on. "C'mon, babe—how?"

"My boss is a good lawyer, but something of a voyeur. Like all good Peeping Toms, he has a telescope. He told me he'd found a 'hunk' for the secretaries, so I looked." She checked for response. "Sue me. You going to shoot?"

Embarrassed, Lyons holstered the Python.

"Bad timing, huh?" Sherry asked, straightening her collar.

Lyons, too busy admiring her sensuous mouth, didn't hear the question. Pretty and gutsy, he thought. "Great combination."

"What's a great combination?" she asked.

"You and me."

She cocked her head and touched the tip of her index finger to the point of her chin. "At your service sir."

Lyons reached for her; then, remembering the impossible situation, he stopped. "Can I take a rain check?" he asked, taking her by the hand.

Sherry stood, pressing her body against him.

The warmth penetrating his shirt jarred Ironman. Fun challenged duty. She felt so good. The possibility that Sherry's appeal would overpower Lyons grew.

"Sure you want me to go?" The obvious danger of Lyons's involvement, whatever it was, excited the compliant brunette. She wanted more.

"N-not now, baby—" Her lips found his before he could finish.

Fire replaced duty.

She reached around behind his head, running her fingers through his hair, and held him in a lover's vise.

Tongues slipped through willing lips to touch. Duty fought for its place in Ironman's conscience.

They ended up on the bed, with Lyons placing the Python on the floor beside it. Four willing hands worked in hasty concert to remove any barrier to greater intimacy.

Soon Lyons was kissing and caressing Sherry's breasts, nuzzling her erect nipples.

Milliseconds before they joined in the waiting ecstasy, the direction finder sounded.

Its insistent beep penetrated Lyons like a cold steel lance. His muscles bunched to help him leap off the bed.

"Noooo," Sherry moaned, trying to capture him with both her arms and legs.

True to his nickname, the Ironman tore himself away from a lovely woman to return to duty. In two strides he had the DF in his hand and was scanning south.

"I don't believe it," the disappointed brunette complained. "I'm competing with a damn beeper."

Lyons, with some difficulty, pulled on his shorts, operating the DF at the same time.

"You're not getting away with this, you know."

Ironman didn't hear her.

She retrieved her panties and threw them at Carl. They landed on the DF. Without looking up, he flicked them away and continued trying to dress and scan at the same time.

"They're closer. Gotta go." He set the electronic device down and finished pulling his pants on. Then, just as if someone had stabbed him in the ribs, he stopped and looked at Sherry, walked over to her, touched her hair and kissed her.

"Sorry, babe. No choice." He took her chin in his callused hand. "Later, after this business is over, can we pick up where we left off?"

"Do you really want to?"

"More than you can imagine."

Pulling his arm until his lips were in range, Sherry kissed him. "Call me." She watched him strap on his weapon, put on his coat and rush out.

"You owe me a second dinner," she shouted at his disappearing back.

Lyons raced down the stairs to his car. The signal got louder. He hit the parking lot at a dead run, listening as he fished out his keys. Once inside the car, he put the device on the seat with the gain as high as it would go. In fifteen seconds he was parked, engine idling, near a freeway entrance.

"Colonel Ziyad Razul, you're going to pay for what you just cost me."

The beep peaked in frequency, then started falling off. "Time to get on their ass," Lyons said out loud. His gray Citation growled its resentment at being driven so hard but responded by placing Lyons on the freeway just four cars behind Allah's Blade's Mercedes and two behind the Horde's Cad.

One man rode with Genghis. Light traffic allowed an easy track. Ahead, the yellow Mercedes took the Johanson exit. The black Cadillac slowed to turn.

Glancing in his rearview mirror, Lyons noticed a blue Ford Bronco slowing to match his pace. Seated in the front were three Latinos who wore the same red headbands as Genghis and his passenger.

16

Comrade Captain Stefan Popov had always been a little claustrophobic, and the Alpha-class submarine's restricted space didn't help. He couldn't stop sweating. He'd been on dozens of training missions involving underwater lockouts and aircraft drops to rafts and high-speed attack boats, but being trapped inside the steel cylinder scared him.

The sub commander leaned against the bunk, well aware of Popov's rising fears after the long voyage. "Well, comrade, what do you think of our little tour boat?"

Popov wiped at his perspiration with a saturated handkerchief. "Stifling, to say the least, but under such difficult conditions—excellent." One didn't advance to captain by alienating the commander of the underwater attack fleet.

"Would you like to join me in the wardroom? The involvement might take your mind off the sardine-can syndrome." The skipper chuckled.

As they entered the tiny space set aside for daily political indoctrination, the *zampolit*, with the arrogance typical of political officers, remained seated.

A weasel hidden in a man's body, he was responsible for the communist training and political health of the entire submarine. He was a member of the KGB, the

Soviet equivalent of the old German Gestapo. He reveled in the fear he generated in the crew.

"Ah, Comrade Captain Popov. Welcome to the real world of heroes." He looked at the small spiral notebook he held. "I see you've been chosen to head a special strike force. Congratulations."

Popov curbed the retort that was trying to escape his lips. He nodded. "Thank you. It's an honor to serve the *Rodina* in any capacity."

The *zampolit* slammed his notebook on the wardroom table. "I shall attend your daily political training lectures with anticipation, comrade—great anticipation. We shall see how well you uphold our great motherland's honor." He stood and forced his way past the pair of commanders.

"He pulls that shitty bullying tactic on every newcomer. Nasty little bastard," the sub commander observed. He shrugged helplessly. "We must live with it."

IN THE CREW QUARTERS of the sub, the team, like soldiers the world over, were trying to guess what their mission was.

"Whatever it is, it's got to be big for them to send a captain as mission leader," Ivan, the group's medic and explosives expert, offered. A stocky Ukranian, he'd cross-trained for combat duty in Afghanistan, patching up soldiers and blowing up civilians.

"If a hero's medal is a possibility, it's got to be a tough target," a wiry Mongolian sitting cross-legged on the floor decided. He brightened. "That's why they chose us—the best of the best."

A murmur of agreement flowed through the group. An oppressive silence fell heavily as each warrior sorted out his feelings. Knowing that they were the cream of the *Moskya Pekhota*, the Russian naval infantry, they never considered the possibility of defeat.

The sub silently made its way toward its target.

17

"I don't understand why we have to go through another test," Alonzo Black whined from the front seat. "We already zapped a supertanker full of oil. What the hell else can I do for an encore, eat an oil field?"

"We hope that's not necessary, but the Brotherhood is very cautious. How is it you say in America? Seeing is believing?" Razul asked.

"Two hundred and fifty-three thousand tons of crude oil ought to be seeing—and believing," the technician complained.

With more patience than he'd ever before demonstrated, the colonel tried again. "Suppose we wanted to fool someone. Couldn't we have staged that shipload of ruined oil? Couldn't the CIA have set that up to draw out the revolutionary groups in America?"

"The CIA wouldn't do such a thing."

Everyone else in the Mercedes burst into raucous laughter. "And your famous red-suited Santa Claus still visits you every Christmastime, too, doesn't he," Tabina prodded.

"They wouldn't," Black insisted.

Razul's rage blocked his reason. Tabina touched him on the arm. Counseling him in Arabic, she warned, "Not yet, Father. We're not finished."

"Sir," said Akmet, "I think Johanson is our turn-off. It's coming up. You might want to confirm with Genghis."

"Allah's Blade to the Horde, next exit. Allah's Blade to the Horde, next exit."

"Roger, Slick Sword," Genghis answered over the radio.

"What does he mean, Slick Sword?" Ziyad wondered.

"It's just his sense of humor."

A red flush crept up her father's neck. "I see. You understand how these street hooligans think, eh? Maybe you want to be one of them." His clenched fists told her to tread lightly.

Speaking in Arabic, his daughter purred, "Beloved father. There is no one on earth I'd rather be with than you. Your cause is my cause, your needs my needs." She brushed his cheek with her fingertips. "You are my past, present and future."

Colonel Razul closed his eyes and tried to blank out the scene he'd witnessed between his daughter and the Chinese hood. Gradually his love for her turned the picture to gray, and his breathing returned to normal.

"We are a team, you and I," he murmured in their native tongue. "A perfect team."

The radio squawked, "Horde to Allah's Blade, Horde to Allah's Blade, we have a negative contact."

Ziyad changed from father to fighting man. "Define target, Allah's Blade out."

"It's Lyons, that ex-cop from L.A. that hassled me in La Jolla. He's two car lengths back."

"How many passengers?"

Genghis laughed. "It looks like the Lone Ranger rides again. He's alone."

"And your new team?"

"They can count the hairs on the back of his neck."

"Solution obvious. Allah's Blade out."

"Horde to rear guard. Step on gray Citation in front of you." Genghis's order crackled over the radio.

STILL ON THE FREQUENCY Schwarz had set, Lyons heard the Horde's transmission.

"Gonna step on me, huh?" he answered looking into the rearview mirror. "Your shoes ain't big enough."

The Mercedes and Cad were already on the off-ramp before Ironman could deal with the Bronco closing on him. Three red-headbanded Latinos pointed out how much trouble he was in. Just in case the rest of Able Team was close, he transmitted his position and problem.

Almost no banking had been built into the off-ramp. Lyons's Citation squealed as he put the pedal to the metal. "C'mon, baby, give me all you've got," he murmured cajolingly.

The Mercedes turned into the tree-lined entrance to a large estate. A massive iron gate swung open automatically as the yellow car approached. The black Cad followed.

I may be setting myself up for an ambush, thought Lyons, but what the hell. He turned into the driveway. Again he transmitted his position to Able Team.

Pressing close, the three Horde members in the blue Ford Bronco were obviously concentrating only on fulfilling their deadly mission. The Bronco pulled up on his left side, forcing Lyons off the road, barely missing a power pole. The punk riding shotgun pointed a sawed-off 12-gauge at the Ironman's head. Convinced his victim was dead meat, the gunner took time to grin at Lyons before he fired.

Instead of matching power against power, Ironman decided to carry aikido principles into the fine art of car-bashing. He pulled off in the direction the Bronco was pushing him, backed off the gas, cramped the wheel and hit the brakes. His Chevy responded like a champion cutting horse. It jerked slightly, then pivoted in a complete circle, ending up on the driver's side of the blue Ford.

Slugs from the double-barreled gun raked the Citation's windshield and hood but missed Lyons. Confused by the sudden maneuver, the Bronco's driver hit the brakes.

"Come and get it." Ironman's Python barked twice.

Surprise became the driver's last expression on earth and his first in hell. The .357 Magnum's blast slammed through the door, spreading out just enough to hit the punk's heart and lungs. He slumped over the steering wheel.

The Bronco lurched and then accelerated; then the front wheels locked. The middle Latino grabbed the steering wheel in time to keep the Ford from rolling as the former driver's remains fell against him. The Bronco shuddered to a stop. The blood-spattered partners sat still for a moment, not believing their friend had been slaughtered. Dignity forgotten, they abandoned the vehicle.

Lyons bailed out of his Chevy. He waited for fire. Either they're setting me up or they dragged their little asses out of the heat. I'll bet they're gone, he told himself, running from the cover of his car to the Bronco. Nothing. He slid around to the right side. The door was swinging. Ironman jumped into the opening, Python ready. Only the dead driver remained, his left arm caught in the steering wheel.

Quickly Lyons checked the area for Genghis. He couldn't believe the Horde's chief would stand by and let Able Team take out more of his members.

He was right.

A screech of tires gave an early warning. Lyons turned in time to see the black Cad bearing down on him. A gunner hung out of the right front window, his Uzi hosing the Bronco's front end.

Ironman dived underneath the death rain and fired back at the Cad. His .357 Magnum roared twice, penetrating the upper windshield and exiting the roof.

A hot slug burned a streak across the Able Team warrior's thigh as the Cad sped by. Genghis, firing a four-pound Israeli Desert Eagle ACP, was hitting close. His slugs plowed four other grooves in the asphalt next to Ironman's head.

Hot bits of black macadam flew into Lyons's eyes, blinding him. He fought the desire to claw away the pain. He brushed his eyes lightly with his fingertips. Then he attempted to induce tears by pulling on his eyelids, but nothing helped. Increasing pain prevented him from touching the lids.

The sound of crunching gravel penetrated Lyons's dark world of pain. He slid his hand across the warm pavement to locate his Python.

"Well, well, well. What have we here? A blind pig?" A hard kick in his side made Lyons grunt.

Carl Lyons tried desperately to open his eyes. He couldn't. Someone took his arm and dragged him out from under the Bronco.

"Did our strong policeman get dust in his little eyeballs?" Another kick landed in his ribs.

Lyons didn't recognize any of the voices.

"Lookie here, Genghis," a second voice heckled as Lyons's .357 clattered across the blacktop. "The nice man lost his iron snake."

"Be a nice boy and give him his Python back," ordered a voice that the blinded Able Team commando recognized instantly.

Pol spoke with deadly authority.

"Take him out," Genghis barked, tugging Lyons toward the Cad.

Schwarz stepped out from behind a eucalyptus tree, fired twice and rolled away. His slugs caught the shotgunner in the lower abdomen, shattering his pelvis.

The Latino's husky body refused to support him. He looked down, watching his own slow-motion collapse. His right hand released the sawed-off 12-gauge. It caught on his index finger, pointed toward his feet and fired, the weight of the weapon pulling the trigger. His right foot disappeared as the shotgun cartwheeled through the air.

Trying to return Gadgets's fire, the Horde members allowed Pol to move in.

"Over here," he yelled.

They turned back toward the source of his voice. Pol aimed at the back of Mok's head. He fired as the Horde's warlord turned.

One FJ parabellum entered the Chinese hood's temple and the other his forehead. Scrambled brains exploded into a bright red mist. The top of his skull flew through the air. He was firing when he was hit, and his Colt Peacemaker barked. One of his shots nicked Genghis in the right heel.

"Son of a bitch," he yelled. "I'm hit." The Horde's chief clung to Ironman, still trying to drag him to his car.

Three rounds from Gadgets's Beretta ricocheted off the macadam near the big Chinese gang leader's head.

"Fuck you bastards," he yelled, squirming to his feet, using Lyons as a shield. He staggered back to the Cad, pressing his Desert Eagle against Lyons's temple. He slid under the steering wheel, still holding the blinded Able Team leader hostage.

"Shoot," Ironman commanded. "Forget me. That's an order." He swung at his captor's head and was struck on the side of the face for his efforts.

Both Pol and Gadgets knew that Lyons's safety was far more important than capturing a street punk. They held their sights on Genghis, waiting for the right moment. Lyons came first.

After starting his car, Genghis backed up slowly, forcing the Able Team warrior to stagger along with him. When he was in position to move out in a hurry, the wounded hood fired at Gadgets, then at Pol.

Ironman tore himself loose, yelling, "Shoot now, you candy-asses." He flattened himself on the blacktop.

Still afraid Genghis might stop long enough to hit Ironman, the other Able Team members held their fire. The black Cad spun its tires, rounding the corner to freedom.

Genghis roared down the private road and into a courtyard. He squealed up to the Mercedes. Allah's Blade and Alonzo Black stood in a group on the steps of the mansion.

"Where the hell were you when I needed you?" he raged, limping over to them. "You heard the shots. They wasted Mok."

As calm as a general in a debriefing session, Razul answered, "The Horde was supposed to be comprised of hardened professionals. We heard the shots, but it never occurred to us that six men couldn't handle one gunner."

"We can handle Lyons. We were ambushed."

"Professionals don't get ambushed."

Genghis spit on the ground in front of Colonel Razul's feet. "I need medical attention. Tabina, drive me."

Razul refused, but, seeing his daughter's quick response, he bit down on his resentment.

The wounded Chinese hood got into the back of the Cad, put his foot up on the front seat and lit a joint. "We'll be back when I locate Lyons."

As they neared the killing ground, Genghis warned Tabina, "They may still be around. Put your foot down as you pass the Bronco."

CONCERNED WITH Ironman's condition, Pol and Gadgets ignored the streaking Cad as it flew by.

"Let the punk run. Down the road we'll get him. At least we have Carl," said Pol.

Lyons tried desperately to sort out the sounds. Helplessness wasn't part of the freedom fighter's job description. Blindness would have to wait. Too many terrorists needed exterminating.

"Hold still, chief," Pol admonished him. "I want to take a quick look at your eyes."

As the medical expert of the group, Pol had the respect of the rest of Able Team. Years of combat experience in Nam had made him an expert emergency medical technician. With the gentleness of a nurse and the precision of an eye doctor, Pol examined his friend.

"A lot of grit and some minor burns. A quick visit to an ophthalmologist should get you cleaned up in a hurry." But Pol pressed his lips together and shook his head at Gadgets.

"I'm not going to be blind?" Lyons questioned.

"I don't think there'll even be any permanent damage. Besides, the eye is the quickest-healing portion of your body. Let me get the biggest pieces out and relieve your pain a little."

Gadgets brought up the car and helped Lyons into the back seat. "Easy, guy. We'll have you patched up in no time. In fact, we can fill you in on the bugs on the way to the doc."

"How'd your mission go?" Lyons asked. "Manage to plant anything?"

Schwarz couldn't resist clowning. "Is the pope Catholic? Does Kurtzman like his computer? Has—?"

"That's enough bullshit," Ironman said in a low whisper. "Give me a yes or a no."

Gadgets winced. "Yes, sir. The mission went fairly well. We were able to bug room 202 but couldn't find the rest of the Brotherhood. How did your tracking go? Was Allah's Blade with Genghis?"

Lyons winced. "I picked them up right outside, but they had a third-car backup, and by the time I got by them Allah's Blade had traveled past the limit of the DF's range."

"Who was the other backup?" Pol asked.

Shrugging, Ironman pursed his lips. "Looked like a trio of Horde soldiers. I nailed one, and the other two made themselves scarce. Then the black Cad returned."

"If you hadn't broadcast your position you might have gone down," Pol said.

"No substitute for good procedure," Lyons agreed.

"After the sawbones, what?" Blancanales asked.

"Maybe we should park within the DF range of the boys in the Sea Star Motel and listen to our new bug at the same time," suggested a quieter Gadgets.

"We should be able to find the location of the rest of their team," Ironman said. "Pol, use your car. Mine's been trashed. I may have been reported to the local police." He didn't mention Sherry's visit.

Within ten minutes they were at the emergency ward of a local hospital. Immediately Lyons had his eyes irrigated and the foreign matter removed. The streak on his thigh only required a touch of antiseptic.

"How bad is he?" Gadgets asked Pol as soon as they were alone.

"Pretty badly burned. It will require hospitalization for a week, at least."

"Ironman doesn't like captivity."

"This is one time Lyons can't bully his way out. If he doesn't take care of his eyes he'll lose his sight."

"I hope someone can convince him of that," Schwarz observed. "The free world can't afford to lose a warrior like Ironman."

18

A squeaking wheel on a food cart signaled that it was mealtime. Orderlies on their way to prep patients for surgery argued about the Los Angeles Raiders' chances. A call for Dr. Blanski in OR 5—code blue—was repeated over the public-address system. Antiseptic odors from room and patient scrubbings permeated every corner.

Carl Lyons was committed to helping the oppressed, the downtrodden, the victims. Now he'd crossed over— he was the one who needed help.

Almost.

A blind warrior was still a warrior. He had not lost his will to fight for what he believed was right.

Only one contact remained with his profession. When he had relinquished his weapons, Lyons had managed to filch a single round of .357 ammunition. He knew it would be hard to feel like a warrior when he was wearing a hospital nightgown designed to barely cover his ass.

The door to his room opened, and as Lyons moved to sit up, Dr. Reinberg ordered, "Lie still, Mr. Johnson. Reduced activity is advisable for a few days. I'd rather you don't disturb those bandages. Nurse Buglisi will be in charge of your care. See that you obey her. I'll check in on you later," he said as he retraced his steps to the hall.

For a freedom fighter who had spent his life in the trenches, the inevitable result of inactivity was guilt. Ironman felt guilty. He started running his actions over and over in his mind.

What if I hadn't taken cover under the truck and just stood to fire at the black Cad? What if I hadn't been messing around with Sherry and had jumped on Allah's Blade sooner? What if I'd gone with Schwarz instead of sending Pol?

What if Hal Brognola—? He suddenly realized he hadn't checked in with Stony Man.

Nurse Buglisi was very obliging when Lyons asked for a phone. He had little choice but to let her dial the call.

He sniffed the brass casing of the .357 cartridge as he waited for the call to connect. Gun oil—the warrior's cocaine, he thought.

Inside three minutes Ironman was talking with Stony Man. Both the Bear and Cowboy were there with Brognola.

"Talk to me, Ironman. How goes it?" Brognola asked.

"I've had better days." Lyons rubbed the brass casing against his forehead.

"I'll buy that," the big Fed answered. "How are your eyes? Any news yet?" Brognola knew the answer. He'd already talked to Dr. Reinberg.

"They tell me that in about three days I'll be able to take the bandages off. Then they'll know if there's any permanent damage. Right now it's kind of iffy." He tried moving the shell between his fingers the way he'd once seen a magician do with a silver dollar. He dropped it on the blanket. A sense of helplessness surged through the Able Team warrior. He desperately searched for his anchor with reality—the round. He found it under a fold of the sheet.

As Brognola talked to Ironman, Aaron Kurtzman, guessing Lyons's anxiety, sat quietly. It was obvious that memories were boiling to the surface, reminding him of the day he had become partners with a wheelchair for the rest of his life. He nervously rubbed the wooden armrests, clearing his throat twice.

Brognola knew the Bear might have more to say to Lyons than the rest of them. He pushed the telephone speaker around so that it faced Aaron.

"Ironman."

"Yeah."

"Kurtzman here."

"Mmm."

The Bear lowered his head. "This may mean nothing at the moment, but things could be a lot worse."

"Yeah. I could be deaf, too." Lyons fingered the .357 round.

"What I mean is, we can still work together, no matter what."

"That's a good one, Aaron. What would I do? I could teach my replacement how to fieldstrip an M-16 in the dark."

The Bear's chair rolled closer to the speaker. In a low voice that came close to breaking, he said, "Look, Carl, we're both warriors. We've both been wounded. We have a place in this battle."

Lyons didn't reply. Holding the phone with his cheek, he rolled the shell back and forth between his palms.

"Even if you lost your sight or had it diminished enough to take you out of combat, your knowledge of antiterrorist warfare is invaluable. Don't cop out."

Touching the cartridge with the tip of his tongue, Ironman tasted bitter gun oil. Without realizing it, he was shaking his head. Lyons stopped, remembering the doctor's orders. He fingered the back of the cartridge, holding it as gently as if it were a lover's hand.

"You still there?"

"Yeah, Bear. I'm still here."

"You disagree with what I've said?" Kurtzman needed a positive answer.

"Yes and no."

The Bear took a deep breath, his eyes closed. When he spoke, it was with the voice of a man who remembered more pain than he wanted to admit. "What is it you don't buy?"

Ironman recognized the hurt in Kurtzman's voice. "I don't buy that I'm going to need special treatment. I'll be out of here in three days—with my Colt."

"I see you still got Ironman's balls." Aaron chuckled. "Get well. We're betting on you."

Brognola cleared his throat. "Enough of this get-well bullshit. Bring me up to speed, Carl."

A grin as wide as a toothpaste salesman's split Ironman's face. For the next half hour Lyons and Brognola covered every possible facet of the situation with Allah's Blade and the Brotherhood.

Exhilarated by the involvement, the Able Team warrior promised to stay out of action until the doctor released him. If he managed to do so, it would be a first. He hung up the phone and laughed, holding the brass .357 cylinder between his index finger and thumb. "Well, old buddy, we'll both be seeing action before this week is out."

IT WASN'T LONG before Hal Brognola was on the phone again, this time with Blancanales. Pol's previous call to the Farm had alerted the Fed to Lyons's injuries and identified the doctor. After Pol gave him his opinion of Ironman's condition, Brognola went silent.

Brognola was more concerned than he wanted to show. "You sure he's okay? He sounded a half-step off when he called in."

"They medicated Carl to relieve the pain. He might be a bit blurred. His eyes have to be bandaged for at least three days. The doctor told Carl he would recover completely, but it'll be three days before any real diagnosis can be made."

"How do you see the Allah's Blade-Brotherhood operation? What does this do to it?"

"We need help. If the Brotherhood buys this bacteria shit they're out of here fast."

"Where's Schwarz now?"

"Outside the Sea Star Motel, listening. We have a beeper in an AK stock and a mike in Omar Khalid's room."

"How about Cowboy Kissinger? Will he fit this operation?"

Blancanales didn't hesitate. "You betcha. Once we get all of these nuts in one sack, nothing's left to do but take the bacteria away from them. He's hand-tailored for firefights."

"Thanks, Pol," Kissinger interjected.

"He'll be there on the next flight," Brognola promised.

"Tell him to come loaded."

"Rosario..."

"Sir?"

"I can't tell you how big this one is. If the process for manufacturing this bacteria gets into the wrong hands, it could be worse than the H-bomb. I've asked for help to contain it."

"Help?"

"Help, but not interference. The FBI has encircled the target area."

"Are you sure about this?" Pol asked.

"This one's too dangerous to chance. I'm not saying I don't think you can't handle it. You can."

"Able Team has always wrestled its own snakes."

Brognola sensed some resentment. "Look, Pol, we must have backup, that's all. Something happened to Ironman, didn't it? You invincible?"

Rosario Blancanales sighed. "Okay, you're the boss. You got it. I'll pick up Cowboy at the airport."

"This is your show," the big Fed promised. "If the Feebies get involved, it'll be at your request. Remember, the White House is watching this one closely. I'm in direct contact with the President."

"Able Team will complete the operation."

19

"Strange wound."

"I don't know how strange it is, doc, but it hurts."

"How did you get it?"

The direction of the questioning bothered the big Oriental. He winked at Tabina. "Working on a concrete hauler and slipped into the ring gear. It chewed the heel off my shoe. We got it out before it ate the rest of my foot."

"Another quarter of an inch and you'd likely have a permanent limp. Come back in a week and I'll remove those stitches. Try to keep your feet out of the machinery. I'll send someone in to bandage it for you." The intern hustled off to the next emergency.

A nurse painted the area and added a gauze pad. "Have you had a patient in here today with asphalt in his eyes?" Genghis asked.

"We sure did. Friend of yours?"

"Not really," Tabina answered. "We promised some friends we'd check on him." She shrugged. "Forgot his name."

The nurse, a pert little brunette with an oversize white winged hat, smiled. "You wait here. I'll peek at the computer. We haven't been too busy. Should be easy."

Within two minutes the nurse was back. She handed Genghis a piece of paper. "Room 317, name's Johnson—William Johnson."

The Chinese hood limped to the elevator. After pushing the button, he leaned against the wall and closed his eyes.

"You all right?"

"Yes. I was just contemplating what we should do with Lyons."

"When are we going to give this imperialist our blessings?"

"Now."

They slipped into Ironman's room.

"Who's there?" the ex-LAPD cop asked.

The mean end of an Israeli Desert Eagle .357 magnum ACP pressed against his neck.

"You cost me four good men. You're going to pay."

Lyons didn't admit that he'd heard or felt anything.

Genghis shoved the automatic harder against his neck. "Pay attention. On your feet, pig." Tabina found a nerve behind his clavicle and squeezed, sending a crippling numbness through his body.

"Fuck you." Consciousness slipped.

"I can't apply any more pressure. He'll pass out," Tabina warned.

"Go out and hustle me an orderly and a gurney. We'll have to do this the hard way."

The Desert Eagle came down hard on Ironman's head.

A SLOW WHISTLE failed to find a tune. The continual slap of a swagger stick striking the palm of a hand telegraphed Colonel Ziyad Razul's mental state.

"Personal vengeance has no place in this operation."

"Until it interferes with your mission, it's none of your business."

The whistle stopped. The swagger stick hesitated. Trapped, Razul thought. I need this infidel dog, but I can't back down in front of my daughter.

"You're wrong, but if my daughter approved the taking of this government operative I'll accept it. We should exploit him."

"Exploit?" Genghis asked, hiding a smile.

"He must know something we don't."

"Ask him when he comes to," the Chinese hood suggested.

AN INSISTENT THROBBING hammered Ironman's head. A Libyan terrorist dressed in the Soviet flag was driving pitons into the inside surface of his skull. After each anchor proved solid he'd climb a little, then stop and drive a piton into another crack. A sudden cold wind came up and almost blew the climber off the face of the cliff.

The chill persisted. Lyons tried to open his eyes. An obsidian blackness wrapped in pain greeted him. He remembered Genghis. Slowly the pieces came back together. Wherever he was, it wasn't a hospital.

Ironman remembered hearing Genghis hassle Razul. I'll have to keep those two at each other's throats, he thought. Maybe their games will provide the break I need. Tabina might be the catalyst for a hell of a fight, he reasoned.

By moving slightly, Lyons confirmed that he was on a sofa with his face turned into the corner between the cushions and the back. He was probably in a motel, which meant they wouldn't be staying long. Lyons felt the sofa sag as someone sat down.

"He's still out," reported Tabina. "Want me to wake him, Father?"

"No. It's too close to six o'clock. We have to meet the Brotherhood's representative in an hour. He's blind and tied up. Leave him where he is. We can pick him up later if we need him."

Lyons heard something move through the air as Razul tossed his swagger stick to his daughter. "See if he reacts."

Tabina stood to swat Ironman across the ass. She held the swagger stick with both hands and swung.

Genghis grabbed her arm, blocking the blow in midswing. "No."

Wide-eyed, she turned to her father.

Razul, challenged again, wondered how much more arrogance he could tolerate. "Why not?" he asked, barely able to speak. Boiling rage threatened to burst his control. "He's our enemy. He should taste hatred. When we're gone, the memory of who's in charge will work to our advantage."

"Bullshit." Genghis cocked the hammer of his ACP and sighted on Ziyad. "Any pain that pig feels will come from me."

Confused, Tabina froze.

"Why are you pointing your weapon at me? You are my employee, are you not?"

His daughter moved toward him.

"Stay where you are, little girl, or I'll waste the good colonel."

"Genghis. Think about what you're doing."

The Chinese smiled, but the knife scar on his left cheek turned a vivid red. "Lyons is mine. *Mine!* I'll decide what he does or doesn't do."

"Why are you so angry?" Razul asked.

"Don't interfere with my revenge—ever."

Colonel Razul shrugged. "You're acting hysterical. I also believe revenge is the sweetest gift. What do you plan to do with him?"

"He's going to learn to beg for death. For now I'll keep him in the trunk of my Cad. Remember—he's mine."

The telephone rang.

Only Omar Khalid knew where the Allah's Blade terrorists were.

Ziyad answered carefully. Quickly he engaged in a heated conversation that ended with him cursing in Arabic. He set the phone down with the precision of a bomb disposal expert. He continued to look at it as though it might explode.

"What's wrong, Father?"

"I think I made a big mistake." He ran the middle finger of his left hand up and down his nose. "By all that is holy, I think I gave away our bacteria."

Everyone in the room, including Carl Lyons, waited for his explanation.

Desolate, Colonel Razul dropped into an overstuffed chair and held his head in his hands. Immediately Tabina moved to comfort him. Razul shuddered, shaking his head. Without any visible sign, he regained control of himself and turned to the microbiologist, who had been silent to that point.

"Well, Mr. Black, it appears we have no use for you." He turned to Tabina. "You wanted practice? Kill him."

Terror painted the lanky scientist's face chalk white. "Why? Why are you doing this?" Tears filled his eyes and ran down his cheeks and into his beard.

"Because, idiot, I sent a sample to the Brotherhood. They destroyed a small storage tank of refined oil. They saved enough of your bacteria to grow more. All they have to do is get it to one of their own microbiologists."

"You don't understand," the frightened technician said.

"That's the trouble. I do understand. I've destroyed Allah's Blade." He nodded to his daughter again. "Do it."

Alonzo Black dropped to his knees. "Really, you don't understand. They don't have usable bacteria. Nobody does."

In one quick movement, the colonel had the weeping traitor by the hair. He bent Black's head back. "What do you mean?"

"I kept something back."

Ziyad located the pressure point behind the microbiologist's ear. He applied a light touch. "Tell me the rest."

Black winced but continued. "I felt that you might not pay me if you had it all, so I never mentioned a step of the growth procedure."

More pressure from Razul's fingers. "And?"

"If the step I left out isn't accomplished, the bacteria will die within seventy-eight hours."

With all of the force he could muster, Colonel Razul slapped Black with his open hand. The blow knocked Black onto the floor.

"Stop," he screamed. "If it wasn't for me you'd have given it away."

Razul stepped up to kick him in the face, but instead of striking his cowering victim he found himself flying through the air. He landed on the overstuffed chair, recovered and bounded to his feet. Enraged.

For the second time he found himself facing the business end of Genghis's Desert Eagle. "You are stupid.

First you make a deal for something with a clinker in it. Then you try to give your formula away. Then you try to kill the dude with the answer to your problems.''

Razul looked at his daughter.

She cocked her head, trying to indicate that there might be some truth in what the big Chinese had said.

"He cheated me," Razul muttered, like a little boy trying to find an excuse to appease his mother.

"You touch him again and I'll blow your head off your body. Dig?" Genghis asked.

"Get up," he ordered Alonzo Black. "Give the rest of your formula to Razul."

"But he'll kill me as soon as he has it," he whined.

"Not as long as I'm here."

Afraid of everyone and everything, the microbiologist described the missing step and wrote the necessary data down.

As soon as he had the paper in his hand, Razul called his Santa Barbara contact to give him the news. By the time he'd finished ridiculing Omar Khalid on the phone, his former arrogance had returned.

"Oh, yes," Razul said, sneering, "if you can find it, the meet at the dolphins is still on." Chuckling, the commander of Allah's Blade hung up.

THREE MILES AWAY, two FBI agents checked out an ambulance with blood on the windshield.

"Driver's dead. Shot with a cannon," the agent in charge confirmed.

"Better check in." The older man pointed at the body with his notebook. "They should know that Carl Lyons has been kidnapped."

The supervisor laughed. "Now we have our own reason for being in on the case."

Scratching his bald head, the older operative looked up from his notes. "Looks like they took him to their safe house and then dumped the ambulance—and the driver."

"Inform the locals, and I'll check in," said Howie Pelendo, the FBI's most highly commended agent.

Howie was called "Eggs" by all his friends; he'd gotten the nickname by always ending up at the top of any group he studied with. Back in junior high school a friend had started calling him "Egghead." Somewhere down the line the "head" had been dropped. During his security investigation before joining the FBI, the name had popped up again, and graduating at the top of his class at the academy had revived it forever.

Eggs was also a gifted athlete, and he never passed up an excuse to run. He sprinted to the public telephone.

20

Conscious, and more angry than uncomfortable, Ironman chafed in the trunk of Genghis's Cad. He decided to remove the bandages. Carefully he peeled the tape from his cheeks and forehead. Even after it had been pulled off, he kept his eyes closed.

All right, Lyons, time to step up and be counted—man or candy-ass. Can you take the answer? he asked himself. You betcha, he replied silently. Anybody who claims to be a champion of the innocent has to have the balls to take what comes down.

Lyons opened his right eye a fraction. Total darkness. A falling sensation started in his throat and ended in his gut. He closed his right eye.

Going for broke. Ironman opened his left eye the same amount. The trunk remained black. He closed his left eye.

Bye-bye combat, hello Stony Man, he thought, remembering Kurtzman's speech about being useful. I hope they can convert antiterrorist information into braille, he thought. Lyons replaced the bandage, matching the tape marks by following the sticky trail left by the tape.

UNAWARE of Ironman's trauma, Genghis walked out to Stearn's Pier as an extra precaution. Everything checked out okay. The Horde's chief returned to the dolphin fountain and sat on the curved bench facing the pier. Alone, he pondered the losses the Horde had sustained. Mok, C.C., Roberto, Shanks and Manuel—all wasted by that pig in the trunk. He recalled what he'd read about his namesake, the first Genghis Khan. The Horde's leader hoped to use the same kind of exquisite torture his hero had used against his enemies.

Despite Ironman's despair and Genghis's bitterness over the loss of men, Santa Barbara experienced another picture-postcard sunset. Sea gulls searched diligently for landing places along the harbor.

A large brown station wagon filled with Middle Eastern men pulled into the parking lot.

"More amateurs," Genghis said to the three dolphins. His rage simmered only a cigarette-paper's thickness below the surface. He let them come to him.

Major Omar Khalid approached him. "Before Colonel Razul gets here, I want to be sure we still agree on the final goal of this operation." He extended his right hand.

"Insecure?" the angry Chinese snarled, ignoring his gesture.

Khalid froze. He had been humiliated enough during his encounter with the blond stranger. His ego refused to take any shit from an American street punk.

"Who do you think you're talking to—Chinese garbage?"

Genghis stood, towering over the Arab terrorist. He shoved his right hand into Khalid's waistband and curled his fingers around the man's belt. The short man found himself even with the Chinese hood's eyes.

"I could blow your head off any time I decided to. Unless you want out, shut your fuckin' mouth."

Khalid remained quiet.

"That's better, my man," the gang leader said. He set the major down.

During the disagreement, Lieutenant Fessi and his men had struggled with the decision of whether or not to interfere, but Khalid had folded before they'd made the wrong one.

"Allah's Blade just turned onto State Street. They'll be here in a minute." Genghis sat down again to admire the smallest dolphin.

The tiled benches around the dolphin statue looked like two yellow parentheses. Off to the right, four men who'd come with Khalid waited, ready to pull out hardware. Tabina, Alonzo Black, Genghis and a Horde soldier waited on the side by the pier. Colonel Razul and Major Khalid sat on the other.

Razul concentrated on the fountain. "Well, major, you've seen the bacteria work. What are your feelings about its power?"

"It's the most impressive weapon I've ever seen. Did you bring the inventor?"

"He's the strange-looking man between my daughter and the Oriental."

Khalid's eyes paused on Black, then danced up and down Tabina.

"Are you prepared to pay the fee?" Razul questioned, breaking Khalid's concentration.

"Fifty million, isn't it?"

"Payable immediately following this final proof—in Switzerland."

Major Khalid fished a small book from his pocket and handed it to Razul. "Does this please you?"

After reading it, Razul chuckled and shook his head.

"Do you find something wrong?"

"You're using the same maneuver I set the inventor up with—a fake bankbook. However, in your case it's much too dangerous."

Khalid stopped squeezing his grip-strengthening device. He replied loudly enough for his men to hear. "Are you threatening the Brotherhood?"

What had been a scene with a group of people who seemed to enjoy a Santa Barbara evening at a waterfront park was turning quickly into a potential killing ground. Each of the gunmen readied himself by selecting his first target. The real pros anticipated their second and third.

The orange sunset flickered in Razul's eyes. With blurring speed he grasped Khalid's upper arm and pressed on a meridian point. The major's fingers relaxed, releasing the exerciser. It clattered to the sidewalk.

"Unless you want to terminate this negotiation—and your life—I'd suggest you relax and stop playing games. Nod if you agree."

Khalid tried to smile as though everything were all right. With more difficulty than he would have thought possible, he moved his head up and down.

Razul released the man's arm, picked up his toy and handed it back with a grin. "Let us continue."

One by one the backup people relaxed. A couple in their thirties pushing a stroller stopped to admire the statue. For five minutes the man lectured his wife on the magnificent traits of the dolphin before pushing the stroller past Razul toward Stearn's Pier.

The interruption gave everyone time to settle down.

"Tell me about your target."

Khalid pointed at a drilling platform with a barge and a tugboat nearby. "That is my choice."

"When?"

"Tonight at nine-thirty."

"Transportation?"

"I have two high-speed net-tenders in the Santa Barbara yacht harbor."

Razul nodded and looked around the area. "I have only one more question. Where's Lieutenant Akmet?"

Khalid shrugged. "He's your man." Khalid had missed Akmet, but he hoped that the fact his competitor had failed to show for the final meeting would embarrass him with the Brotherhood.

A squad car pulled up to the small drive-in restaurant. Two men got out and walked toward the take-out window.

Probably just local police, the group decided. Still, none of them felt comfortable. Razul stood. "Akmet's probably back at the hotel. We'll rendezvous at the yacht harbor at nine. He'll be there."

CARL LYONS COULDN'T stop shaking. The temperature had dropped significantly when the sun had gone down. The cold steel of the Cadillac's trunk sucked out Lyons's body heat. He heard the key being inserted in the lock. All his despair, frustration and rage over the loss of his sight combined to spring-load Lyons into combat mode. A whoosh of cold, fresh air swept into the exhaust-filled trunk.

"Keepin' warm?"

"Fuck you."

Genghis squeezed Lyons's jaw hard, talking straight into his face. "Hang in there, hero. After you provide cover for us, I'm going to kill you one inch at a time."

Triggered, the spring-loaded Able Team warrior grabbed the Oriental's wrist with both hands and jerked with a loud *kiai*. The big hood fell into the trunk and onto Lyons.

Lyons tried for Genghis's throat but tasted blood from a right hand to the mouth. He clung to the wrist the way a bull rider holds on to a loose rope.

Most people would find that fighting blind in the trunk of a Cadillac left something to be desired. For Ironman, the first action he'd been able to latch on to since his blinding exhilarated him. Pain or no pain, Ironman lived.

Grunts were all the two combatants uttered. Fists, elbows, foreheads and knees were the implements of the moment.

Genghis backfisted Lyons's head.

Lyons chopped a trapezius.

Ironman's chest burned from a blow meant for his face.

He pulled the long black hair hard enough to peel Genghis off.

The Chinese recovered by applying *hadaka jime*, the unbreakable naked stranglehold of Kodokan judo.

The Stony Man commando correctly ignored the pressure on his throat and tried fighting his way out.

As his blows weakened, Genghis kept his forehead pressed to the back of Ironman's neck.

"Gotcha, asshole," he squeezed out between clenched teeth. "Don't think it ends here."

With the blood and oxygen supply to his brain cut off, the soft veil of darkness slid gently down over Lyons's consciousness.

"You're a tough son of a bitch, pig. I'll give you that," Genghis said as he climbed out of the trunk. He closed the lid and walked around to the driver's seat.

21

"They've got Ironman."

Blancanales held his breath.

"Right out of the hospital."

Lyons captured. He refused to believe it.

"Hal." Blancanales couldn't say any more.

The unique bond that binds all warriors together into a brotherhood stretched, but didn't break. "He's not dead." Blancanales stated it as a fact.

"We don't know that."

Rage, like a deadly plague, infected Pol. "Do you know who took him?"

"Witnesses confirm a beautiful young Middle Eastern female and a big Oriental male."

"Tabina and Genghis."

The possibility that Carl Lyons would be wasted by such scum was unbearable. Too many firefights—too many battles for freedom—had been won by the big blonde for him to be snuffed by a street hood and a terrorist.

"No."

"No, what?" Brognola asked. The top Fed had also been hit hard by the possibility of losing Carl Lyons.

"I don't believe he's dead. Who reported it?"

"The Feebies. They found an ambulance and its executed driver."

"I want their help," Blancanales announced without hesitation. "Plug 'em in."

"Thanks, Pol. I knew you'd see it that way."

"One more thing, Hal. You were right about the Feebie assistance. Sorry."

"Thanks. Incident forgotten. Now go find Carl."

Rosario Blancanales had had to be a killing machine in the jungles of Nam. Tortured children, battered mothers and mutilated fathers had ignited a searching flame in the young warrior's brain, but this involved a partner. A friend.

Ironman. Able Team comrade in the never-ending war to help the innocents. Now the enemy had him.

Blancanales blinked away the dampness in his eyes. "I'm coming, partner. Hang in there."

Gadgets waited impatiently for Pol to complete the call.

"They've got Ironman."

Hermann "Gadgets" Schwarz had always been accused of having a battery for a heart and a computer for a brain but, when he heard the news, whatever he had froze.

"Who?"

"Genghis and Allah's Blade."

Able Team's electronic wizard remained motionless, his eyes closed. When he opened them they were different. They looked like the working ends of 9 mm slugs, gray and deadly. "Well, partner, it's our turn." Gadgets swallowed. "It's rock-and-roll time. Let's kick some ass."

AFTER PICKING UP Cowboy Kissinger, Rosario headed back to the stakeout. Gadgets had obviously made some headway, judging by the look on his face.

"I found the Libyan," he told them before he even greeted Cowboy.

Pol grabbed his arm. "Which one?"

Schwarz pointed down the street. "The leader of the group that hit us at the hotel. Lieutenant Akmet, no less."

"How good is he?" Cowboy asked.

"He may be able to follow specific orders, but he sure as hell can't innovate in an emergency," Pol said. "Let's take him."

"Do you mean hit him or ask him to join us?" Kissinger asked.

"I think a foursome would be delightful," Gadgets offered. "There's no end of things we could talk about."

Rosario's eyes went deadly. "Ironman. That's what we could talk about." The muscles in Pol's jaw twitched. Just the thought of Lyons shifted his memory bank to Nam and the get-it-done days.

"Where did he go?" Blancanales asked.

"He turned in at that 7-11 halfway down the block," Gadgets answered.

"When?"

"Not more than three minutes ago."

"Cowboy, why don't you go get yourself a Coke. While you're at it, see if Lieutenant Akmet is allowed to eat during duty hours," Pol ordered.

Built like a cross between a defensive tackle and an outside linebacker, Cowboy moved as quickly as a rookie receiver with a pissed-off cornerback on his ass. One moment he was in the car, the next he was walking down the street whistling "The Yellow Rose of Texas."

Able Team's weapons expert arrived at the convenience store's parking lot just as Akmet came out through the door. His tweed sport coat bulged slightly near the left armpit. Obviously nervous, Akmet walked in small, quick steps, his eyes constantly scanning the pedestrians. A glance at Cowboy's ten-gallon hat and high-heeled boots immediately removed him from the number of "possibles" within Akmet's view.

"Well, I'll be!" Cowboy threw his brown Stetson at Akmet. "Tariq! Why didn't you tell me you were in town?"

Shock and a quick survey of everyone looking at him confused the lieutenant. He stood still on the step above the parking lot when Cowboy embraced him like a lost brother. Kissinger's chest blocked any possibility of Akmet reaching his 9 mm Browning ACP.

With a large grin, Kissinger whispered, "If you so much as blink I'll blow your head into that sack you're carrying. Smile and shake my hand."

Numb, the terrorist shook with his right hand, thereby removing any chance of his reaching his piece.

"Walk on my left side and chat about the weather."

An elderly couple going the other way smiled at them. Cowboy tipped his hat.

It was just the opportunity Akmet had been waiting for. He quickly slid his hand toward his shoulder holster.

Cowboy's right hand closed around Akmet's upper arm like a shark's jaws. He squeezed harder as the elderly couple continued on into the store.

Never a friend of his own pain, Akmet complied.

"Fun and games are over. Hand me your weapon—now."

"In the open?"

Rather than discuss it, Cowboy reached in and yanked the Browning from its holster.

After losing his automatic, the frightened soldier walked silently to the car. Cowboy told him to close his eyes when they arrived. Akmet was convinced he was going to be taken for a ride, just like in American gangster movies.

Gadgets laughed. "You were gone so long we were going to send out a rescue team."

"Let's get him where I can exercise my gifts," Pol suggested.

THE SMELL OF FEAR mixed with sweat dominated the small hotel room. Lieutenant Tariq Akmet, personal favorite of General Mousa and mole in Allah's Blade, was shaking. Convinced that all that lay ahead of him was torture, then murder, he surrendered all integrity. He knew he couldn't hold out. A secret terror of pain forced bile up into the back of his mouth. The men who'd captured him displayed a special anger, a burning hatred as apparent as the flames in a blast furnace. Sparks touched him every time they looked his way.

"You're dead. You're just not buried yet." Blancanales rubbed his Beretta 93-R. He wanted to hurt the communist terrorist so badly he, too, was shaking. Control, he thought, releasing and reinserting the magazine. I've got to remain under control. What would Ironman do if everything was reversed and I was the prisoner? Get hard, that's what. He'd get down to what had to be done and do it—like the pro he is. The 93-R felt good.

Schwarz leaned against the wall, wrestling with the same problem. He knew Ironman's life depended on the information they extracted from Akmet.

"You look a little tight, Gadgets." Cowboy's emotional state was different. It was not that he didn't care.

He did. A relative newcomer to Able Team and their war against terrorism, he was more detached. He was completely professional, with no emotions to get in the way. His cool would help.

"Rosario. Break is over. Time to rock and roll."

Kissinger said, "You'll need your flanks watched."

Pol nodded, and Cowboy disappeared down the hall.

Able Team had already decided to play "good guy-bad guy" with Akmet. They had already rattled his cage by tying him to the bed, spread-eagled and faceup.

"You are the imperialist scum who killed my men."

Gadgets laughed. "You noticed?"

"You're going to pay, too," spit Blancanales. "Only it's going to take one hell of a lot longer."

"Easy, partner. We want information, not bodies."

Pol stared at Schwarz. "What's with you? I ought to just burn him now." He cocked his Beretta.

Schwarz traced an imaginary circle at his temple, looking at Akmet. As Gadgets moved his finger, the Arab followed with his frightened eyes.

Pretending to be offended, Blancanales eased the hammer down. Without warning, he pulled out a slender Gerber combat knife, slipped the blade under the frightened Arab's belt and cut through the leather. "I'm going to skin him alive."

"Wait a minute. Don't. You haven't even asked him a question yet." Gadgets held Pol's wrist. "Give him a chance. C'mon."

Pol hesitated, as though he were considering the suggestion. "Bullshit." He reached for the prisoner's throat.

"Wait." Before Akmet could say anything else, his stomach convulsed and he puked all over his chest.

"I don't need what this sloppy pig has to say," Blancanales griped, waving his automatic.

Schwarz jumped up and placed himself between Rosario and his intended victim. "Hold it. Why don't you take a break? Let me talk to him. Cool off." He walked his grumbling partner to the door. "Five minutes. Give us five."

"Not a second longer." He glared at the bed and slammed the door.

Gadgets went into the bathroom and wet a towel. He returned and untied Akmet's left hand. Schwarz sat on the bed and watched.

Disgusted with himself, the Muslim wiped up the vomit on his chest, thinking that he should never have decided to become a warrior.

"Well?" Gadgets asked.

"What?"

"Our angry friend will be back in—" he checked his watch "—two minutes. Anything you can tell me that'll keep you alive?"

Bile mixed with fear burned the Arab's nostrils. He felt sick again. His stomach wrenched, but he swallowed his way out of more humiliation. Fists clenched against his fear, Akmet lay motionless, fighting his own private war.

Pol turned the doorknob slowly until the mechanism clicked open.

The noise triggered a miniature explosion of terror that expanded outward from the pit of the officer's stomach in concentric ripples. It reverberated in his brain.

"Well? He's back."

Blancanales pushed the door so hard it slammed into the wall.

Sighing, Schwarz tapped Akmet on the boot. "He's all yours. I tried to make it easy on you. Good luck." He walked toward the door, saying, "Don't forget to gag him. We can't upset the neighbors with unnecessary screaming... you know."

Akmet shrieked, "Wait."

Pol tossed his combat knife into the air and caught it by the blade. He grinned.

"I'll be in the coffee shop when you're through with your... fun."

Pol laughed. "Chicken."

Feigning anger, Gadgets snapped, "How many skinnings do I need to watch to understand what they do? You enjoy this shit too much." He slammed the door and waited in the hall.

Akmet couldn't blink. His eyes locked on the Gerber combat knife. His brain soaked up the conversation. A chill shuddered through his torso.

Pol watched with his back against the door, then moved toward the bed.

A whisper emanated from Akmet. "Drilling platform."

Blancanales held the blade of his knife under the Lieutenant's chin. "What was that?" he questioned.

"Drilling platform, they're going to a drilling platform."

"And?"

The broken officer's lips trembled. "I'll tell you everything if you promise not to kill me."

"What do you mean by 'everything'?"

"Whatever I know... you'll know. Please don't kill me." He wept softly, whispering "Please don't" again and again.

With a flick of his wrist, Blancanales threw the Gerber. It went through the blanket and into the mattress at the other end of the bed. He turned his back and dialed the FBI.

"If you so much as hiccup, I'll end it all." He walked over and rapped on the door.

Schwarz stepped into the room, squinting. His eyes widened. "I thought you were going to do your thing?"

"Our Lieutenant Tariq Akmet decided to, ah ... save his skin, so to speak."

"Listen close," Pol commanded. "We're only going to ask this once. Where's Carl Lyons?"

"He's in the Chinese hood's trunk."

Gadgets grabbed his shirt. "And where's the car, smartass?"

Blancanales broke in. "What kind of condition is he in?"

"He's blind. Wearing bandages on his eyes. I—I didn't do it. I didn't." He wept.

"And where's the car now?" Schwarz demanded, his adrenaline pumping.

"Next to the dolphins."

"Dolphins?" Pol asked. "What the hell are you talking about, an aquarium?"

Before Akmet could answer, the door burst open to reveal Cowboy, accompanied by Eggs Pelendo and two of his men.

"Intersection of State and Cabrillo, right next to Stearn's Pier," Pelendo said.

Pol nodded.

Eggs retrieved his radio from a grinning Kissinger and squeezed the On switch. "Check for—" He looked at Pol.

"Black '87 Coupe de Ville Cad. California license number 1NKE499. Ironman's in the trunk, blind."

Eggs repeated the data and ordered the area surrounded.

22

Shelf Master No. 9, an old drilling rig by West Coast standards, looked like a rusty spider. She'd had her feet stuck in channel mud for more than fifteen years. Even when the big blowout had covered Santa Barbara's beaches with globs of crude, old No. 9 had kept right on producing. Ready for a workover, she struggled to meet her allotment.

Only one man on the Coast could accomplish the job without spilling a drop of oil into Santa Barbara's waters. Buzz Condrona had acquired his nickname early on because of an odd noise he sometimes made when thinking. He'd pull on his lower lip and hum at the same time, emitting a sound identical to that of a kazoo.

A former dryland driller, then a tool pusher on off-shore rigs, he'd been assigned to evaluate and bring the Shelf Master back on-line at a hundred and fifteen percent within three months. The derrick had already been reworked. The geologists believed that total recovery plus a fifteen-percent increase over her previous records was the minimum they could expect.

Buzz had learned early in his career to never trust the technical geniuses. He had to admit, however, that Peeter De Zonderhundt, the project geologist, had earned his respect.

Condrona grumbled about the seven-man crew he'd inherited. "Money hunters," he called them. Desire to be professional oilmen didn't motivate them, but bucks—lots of them—did.

"Worse than rust," he'd muttered after checking them out. Still, Buzz knew his career had blossomed with half-assed men he'd turned into hard-driving workers. Maybe one more time, he thought.

Piece by piece, the drilling equipment arrived. The cranes had never been removed. Now they were kept busy. A barge pushed by a hundred-and-thirty-five-foot tug called the *Pussy Cat* supposedly carried everything the project needed. Another barge was tied up on the leeward side of the rig. Capable of holding sixty thousand gallons of crude, she'd stay there until the well shut down.

"Well, Buzz, what do you think?" De Zonderhundt, known as the "Flying Dutchman" behind his back, asked as he laid his heavy hand on the tool pusher's shoulder.

Always intimidated by six-foot-four-inch size, Buzz glanced at the crew. "I think we've got our work cut out for us. These kids are all balls and no brains. They're willing, but only if it's dangerous."

The Flying Dutchman chuckled. More than once he'd earned his name by using his fists instead of his brains. Battling in bars has always been a part of the rough-neck's job description. He had always migrated to the hangouts with world-class fighters. Instead of avoiding brawls, he watched until his friends were in trouble. Then he launched his massive frame into the air like a muscle missile. Usually the target—or targets—were smashed unconscious by the Dutch ICBM.

The working barge lightly nudged No. 9's support columns. Her deck contained the last of the bigger equipment to be hoisted aboard the platform. A rigger setting a rope sling on a Halliburton signaled the crane operator to raise it. "Watch it," yelled Buzz, "you're not going to have a balanced load. Move it to the right." He waved his hands furiously.

De Zonderhundt laughed. "If he dropped it you'd probably jump down there and catch it."

The crane operator gave Condrona the high sign, took up the slack on the sling and raised the equipment easily. Buzz watched another rigger carefully guide the Halliburton onto the chalk marks.

"Looks like you have visitors," commented the Dutchman, pointing east.

"Shit. I hope it's not more help from my boss. I'll never finish on time."

"Your boss never wore a suit like those guys in his life."

"Can't be tourists . . . can they?"

"We'll know in a minute. They're moving in here like bats out of hell."

"Looks like a small Coast Guard launch. Shit. I'll bet we're in for an inspection. It's too fucking early."

Buzz watched the boat skipper swing alongside the barge. He stopped without banging into the fenders. Coast Guard for sure. The passengers worked their way through the tangle of hardware on the barge.

"They look like hard dudes. Bet they're cops." De Zonderhundt followed Buzz down the ladder to meet the visitors.

"Whatever their business is, they're serious." Condrona's lip was buzzing by the time they reached him.

"You the boss here?" a dark-skinned man asked as he held out his hand.

"Yes."

"We'd like to talk to you in private if possible."

"They call me Buzz. What the hell's the problem? And who are you?"

"I'd rather wait until we're in private, if you don't mind, sir."

The Dutchman turned away. "I'll go check on the Halliburton. Yell if you need me."

Able Team followed Buzz to his office. Totally functional, it obviously belonged to a working manager. Lying in the middle of his desk was a twisted chrome-plated crescent wrench. Buzz always picked it up when he entered his office. A rusted two-inch piece of a kelly from his first gusher served as a paperweight. Stained photographs of previous drilling crews hung at random around the small room. Only one chair and a scribbled note on his green board reflected the all-business attitude of Buzz Condrona. The note read *Semper Fi*, the short form of the Marine motto: Always Faithful.

"No such thing as an ex-Marine," Pol noted.

"You betcha," Buzz agreed, straightening a little.

Gadgets couldn't ignore the battered wrench lying on Buzz's desk. "Tell me about your fancy hardware there," he asked, pointing.

"This is the most expensive wrench in the world. It's worth a hundred thousand dollars."

"Could have fooled me."

"A driller I had to fire threw it down a well when we had the string out. Cost a hundred thou to recover it before we could continue drilling."

"Did you fire the next one in a bar?" Schwarz asked, laughing.

"As a matter of fact, I did. Let's cut the bullshit. What the hell is all of this?" Buzz demanded. "Who are you people?"

With great care, Pol explained the coming battle and the significance of the *R. P. Zinglow* massacre.

Condrona was buzzing by the time Pol finished. He shook his head. "You mean those communists killed all of those sailors just for attention? Must be mean bastards. What can I do to help?"

"Leave," Pol stated.

"Fuck you. This is my rig. If anybody's going to leave it'll be you. I don't run from a fight. Neither do my men."

With the exception of his double tour with the Marines fighting the brown-water war in the Mekong Delta, Condrona's life had been devoted to oil wells. Screw with his rig and you took on Buzz.

"Where did these commies come from?"

"Libya."

"Every man I know would like to have a go at Khadaffi." For the first time, Buzz noticed Kissinger. "Is this guy in the ten-gallon hat one of your team?" He pointed at Cowboy Kissinger's hundred-dollar Stetson.

"Yes, name's Cowboy. What's your answer?" Pol asked. "Will you evacuate?"

The tool pusher thought about his crew and their love of danger. They'd bite the end off an M-16 if he asked. Still, using undisciplined guts without brains was like putting an untrained bull elephant in front of a racing sulky. Everything got smashed. Nobody won.

Buzz's lower lip vibrated.

Gadgets couldn't resist. "That's about a 30-hertz frequency you got there, friend."

He released his lip. "Compromise?"

Blancanales raised his eyebrows.

"How about me and the Flying Dutchman staying behind? We both have combat experience."

"Not a chance."

"Off. Off my rig." Buzz pointed toward the beach.

"We can't do that," Pol replied.

The boss reached for the top drawer of his desk. Before he could get his hand around the ivory butt of his Colt .45, two silenced Beretta 93-Rs and one customized Colt Commander centered on his forehead.

All three Stony Man warriors shook their heads no.

The tool pusher reached for his lip.

Knowing the situation had to have an emotional release, Gadgets trotted out his sense of humor.

"Count 'em. Three, no less than three. For one dime, the tenth part of a dollar, you can take a chance on beating the crazies."

Buzz's glazed eyes told Gadgets that the oil rig's boss hadn't changed his mind. "If you win, you get to fight the Libyan commies all by yourself. However, if you lose, you've seen the last of everything."

Condrona's eyes showed his acceptance of reality. "Three of a kind beats an empty hand. You win." He shoved the drawer shut with his thigh. "What d'ya want?"

"Give us a complete tour of this rig and all of the dangerous places on the oil barge. Then you can evacuate your people with the tug *Pussy Cat*," Blancanales answered.

Buzz sighed and nodded. They started with the helicopter pad. The group followed the subdued tool pusher through the machinery house, past the Schlumberger, the pipe rack, six mud tanks and the mud and cement house and its Halliburton and finally inspected the crew quarters.

"That do it?" Without waiting for an answer, Buzz put his fingers between his lips and whistled for the crew. They gathered by the crane. He invented a story about the Coast Guard and their "chickenshit inspections." They had to evacuate the rig until the next morning.

"How much is this going to cost us?" asked a beer-bellied young man.

"Not a fuckin' cent. Go get laid. Be ready to work your asses off tomorrow."

A ragged cheer and a couple of *all right*s showed their approval. Within five minutes they were on the *Pussy Cat*.

No one noticed that the Flying Dutchman missed the boat ride.

"Let's set up our killing ground and our backup positions," ordered Rosario. "Buzz, why don't you take the Coast Guard boat back?" He stuck his hand out. "Thanks, partner. No hard feelings?"

"Naw. I just wish I could be in on the action. I could pay some debts for friends I lost in the Mekong Delta." He shrugged and jumped into the waiting boat.

"We have two hours to prepare the best meal Allah's Blade, the Brotherhood and the Horde ever ate—a gourmet dinner of FJ slugs with Ironman's name stamped on every one," Pol said.

"I'll bet the Statue of Liberty's torch will burn brighter after nine-thirty than before," Kissinger mused.

"Amen," chorused Schwarz and Blancanales.

23

Aaron Kurtzman's wheelchair remained motionless. The Bear watched as Hal Brognola chomped on his cigar and paced from one end of the room to the other.

"Tough?" asked Aaron.

Brognola, breathing deeply, sighed, "Yeah. The White House is fully aware of the scope of the problem in Santa Barbara." He slammed his fist on the table.

"If only Carl could be rescued."

"He doesn't count in this equation, does he?"

"Not when his life is measured against America's needs."

Brognola understood the situation all too clearly. Men who fought the enemy to save the innocents knew they were expendable. Heroes were often ridiculed by men who, in the name of peace, negotiated away freedoms. Brognola also knew that, for once, he felt totally helpless.

EXPENSIVE FRENCH COLOGNE drifted through the strong smell of soldiers' prebattle sweat. Both double beds and all four chairs were occupied. Lieutenant Fessi and his men stood with their backs pressed against the wall. Folded pizza boxes and crushed soda cans overflowed the wastebaskets. Genghis and Tabina were locked in an intimate conversation on the farthest bed from the table. The last two of the Horde's men lounged against the wall.

Colonel Razul pulled up a chair across the table from Major Khalid. For twenty minutes they waded through typical Arab amenities before getting down to business. Both men could barely control their tempers.

"You have a defector," Major Khalid spit at Colonel Razul. "Our plans must change."

Instead of exploding in rage, Razul laughed. He and his daughter also had a strategy for the meeting.

Stunned by the lack of reaction, Khalid blinked. He had been positive his accusation would generate enough anger to force a confrontation, and he hesitated now.

"How can you consider yourself a commanding officer when your own staff is unstable?" he asked.

Colonel Ziyad Razul chuckled. He raised his eyebrows. He tapped his swagger stick against his boot. He smoothed his mustache. He smiled at Tabina. But this time he didn't lose his temper.

"How can you sit there and grin when Tariq Akmet is, at this very moment, disclosing our plans to the enemy?"

Still ignoring the taunts, Razul practised strengthening his fingers by stabbing them into the opposite palm.

Seated with his injured foot propped up on the TV, Genghis watched the interplay. We're going to have only one Libyan commander after this fracas is over, he thought to himself.

"You incompetent bastard! How you ever gained the rank of colonel is one of the mysteries of the ages." Desperation elevated Khalid's voice to the level of hysteria. He paced back and forth as though he were lecturing at a university.

Khalid shouted at Tabina. "Are you sure he's your father? How could someone as competent as you spring from—" he pointed at her father "—that, that obvious loser?"

During the entire interplay, Alonzo Black cowered in the corner. He could see his money disappearing because of a fight during which the Muslim hotheads killed each other. He hoped Genghis would protect him.

Tabina was well aware of Khalid's obsession with sex and his interest in her, and she knew that the battle had shifted to her arena.

In a split second, Khalid forgot Razul, the bacteria and the Brotherhood. He brushed his gaze over her thin pink blouse. Pausing at her generous breasts, he licked his upper lip.

Tabina moved her shoulders provocatively. Then, with the sensual control of an attacking boa constrictor, she moved her right hand down to straighten her blue miniskirt. Pausing at her flat tummy, she winked.

Licking his lips, Khalid stepped toward her.

Tabina allowed him to pull her to her feet. She touched her hair while slowly moving toward him. The Berber terrorist drowned in her sensual flood. She captured his eyes, locked on to them and smiled. The hook set. Tabina Razul whispered, "Omar," as though his name were sacred.

Despite the fact that this had begun as a ploy to anger Allah's Blade's commander, he was losing his common sense. Major Omar Khalid had never doubted his personal magnetism. He was convinced that no woman could resist him, just as no commando could resist trying out the latest SMG.

Genghis and Alonzo Black watched Ziyad.

Swagger stick at rest, he smiled.

Drowning Khalid with her eyes, Tabina slid her left arm around his back. Yielding, she pulled him to her. Flames were fanned to white heat.

Khalid bent to kiss her.

Showing little interest, her father counted the braids on his swagger stick.

Approval painted on their grinning faces, Lieutenant Fessi and the rest of the Libyan team turned discreetly away.

Everyone in the room puzzled over the intensity of Khalid's aggressiveness. Colonel Razul's love for his daughter presented a big enough threat to limit everyone else's interest to wishful thinking. Yet it appeared that Khalid was going to make love to her right in front of her father. It didn't make sense. They watched Razul for signs of anger.

Taking her head in both his hands, Khalid opened his mouth to kiss the compliant woman.

An envelope of pain surrounded him so quickly that he lost his breath. He froze. Excruciating waves radiated from every part of his body. Each one created its own concentric circle. The hurt traveled in circles, growing and shrinking, intersecting, then expanding again. Tears streamed down his face.

With a low whistle of delight, Colonel Ziyad Razul watched his beloved daughter restore the family honor.

She had Khalid in the tiger's-mouth grip with her right hand, and she was moving her left hand around his body with blurring speed. Every time it stopped she attacked another nerve center, adding another pebble of pain to Khalid's pool of agony.

"I'd suggest you remain leaning against the wall, Lieutenant Fessi," Razul ordered, pointing a Browning 9 mm at his head.

"Yes, sir, colonel."

"I knew it," roared Genghis. "I knew she'd show him." He slapped Alonzo Black hard on the shoulder, knocking him out of his chair. "You owe me five bucks. She wiped him out in less than three minutes." The big Chinese hood rejoiced. He was just as taken with her as Khalid was.

OUTSIDE, in a Cadillac trunk, a different pain pressed its victim to the wall. When he stopped to think, Carl Lyons admitted a chill of fear.

Ironman worked at escaping. For a while he tried brute force. The trunk lid curved just enough to allow him to lie on his back and leg-press. His only reward was sweat—and the chance to stay warm. His energy expended, Lyons tried to think his way out. In the absolute darkness he probed, touched every square inch of the luxury car's stripped trunk. After feeling and attempting to disassemble anything that felt as though it might come apart, he rested. He lay back to ponder. His sweat-covered body shifted to a bone-rattling chill.

A trip to Alcatraz flashed through his mind. When visiting the hole, he remembered a tour guide describing cons who'd been stripped naked and placed in isolation for thirty days. To minimize the loss of body heat they'd slept on their knees and elbows. No other part of their bodies touched the steel floor. He tried it.

"This shit works," he said aloud. His voice reverberated in the trunk, restoring his sense of reality. While he was balanced Alcatraz-style, he made a discovery. Even though he had to stretch out a bit to keep his back from touching the lid, the position placed his head at the level of the seam where the trunk met the body. A large truck rumbled by with its lights on. Lyons saw the flash.

Hope welled up in Ironman as if someone had set off a hundred-pound charge of C-4 plastic explosive in his chest.

"Ironman ain't out of it yet, Genghis." He quickly balanced on his knees and on one hand and ripped his bandages, which had come loose, off.

Utter darkness. He tried putting his face close to the crack. Nothing. Despair overcame him.

A car sped by. Kneeling with his head down and his eyes closed, Lyons again sensed the light. He tried jerking his head up and banged it. Another set of lights illuminated the crack. With his eyes open a slit, Lyons saw a turn signal flash.

Exhilarating joy returned. It's a second chance, he thought. Feeling carefully, he retrieved his bandages, but he delayed putting them back on. He had to use his eyes a little more before covering them again. It took every bit of the famous Ironman discipline to keep from bellowing his elation.

He was a patriot returned from the edge. The free world moved one hero closer to deliverance.

MAJOR KHALID WAS still in Tabina's grasp, and only deep breathing could be heard over his moaning.

"Well, Omar, what do we do about your desire to force a confrontation?" asked Razul

The formerly arrogant Libyan commander gulped down his pain and shook his head. Finally he raised his palm and shook it in Razul's face.

Tabina looked to her father for direction. "Enough?"

Razul, unwilling to see this delicious moment end, cocked his head in feigned consideration. "Before you release this amateur, I want the apartment checked for bugs." He scanned the room with his swagger stick and nodded at Lieutenant Fessi.

His men looked at him. "Do it," he ordered. Within a few minutes they had turned the rooms into Early American trash. Fessi forced them to keep looking. One bug was found in the toilet paper roll and two in the telephone.

The transceivers looked like three innocent coins. Ziyad walked around the room, displaying the evidence of Khalid's stupidity for effect. Then he held the units close to his mouth, said, "Allah's Blade out," and smashed them on the table with the butt of his Browning ACP.

"Release the amateur."

All waited quietly for Khalid to regain his wits. He sat, depressed, rubbing his hand. His glowering at Tabina gave her pleasure. She cocked her head at him and smiled sexily. Khalid cursed in Arabic and turned away from her.

"We'll have to change our timing and the place of the test," Razul stated. "Agreed?"

Khalid couldn't keep his mouth shut. "If Akmet had betrayed us we would be in chains or dead by now." He glanced at his watch. "Let's just shift our timing a bit and go now. I still have my backup."

The third time Khalid mentioned his mysterious support registered. Razul, bothered by the possibility of some unknown source of strength for Khalid, held his curiosity in check and promised himself that he would be vigilant.

They filed out and into their respective cars. Genghis thumped on the trunk of the Cadillac as he passed. "Wake up! Time to go to work."

A muffled "Fuck you" squeezed out through the new cracks on the edge of the slightly bent trunk lid.

24

Howie "Eggs" Pelendo sipped his martini as he struggled with the data. Why would the agency pull him away from his cases to baby-sit a secret antiterrorist squad? This mission had to be big. Federal agencies with enough firepower to take on the Army covered the landscape. Why the FBI? And why hands off? Hal Brognola told it straight. He'd lean on him.

Eggs surprised Brognola with his call.

"What's really bothering you?" Hal asked.

"I'm a baby-sitter for a baby that doesn't need me."

"How'd you come to that conclusion?"

"I've seen your men operate."

"Bring me up to date. Anything on Ironman yet?"

"We know where he is, but we've decided against rescuing him at this point. Afraid to tip our hand."

"This is a lousy way to make a living," Brognola growled. "We have to risk our best people to stop a terrorist."

"We could quit," Eggs offered.

"Like hell we could. Until the words *communist* and *terrorist* are only found in textbooks, we work."

"There's a few more you could add. *Mafia*, *yakuza*, *tong*, to name a few," Eggs said.

"I suppose you're right." Brognola sighed. "What itch do you need scratched...really?"

"I want a piece of the action."

"I don't think I can do that." Even though he'd pressed Blancanales to use the FBI, Brognola hesitated. Screwing with Able Team's chemistry might have bad consequences. He decided to give Eggs limited access but make him negotiate for it.

"Why?"

Brognola remembered the sound of Pol's voice when he'd responded to orders that included accepting help from the Feds. "It wouldn't go down well with my men."

An extended silence told Stony Man's boss that Eggs's computer-fast mind was searching for some rationale for joining the operation.

Brognola took the initiative. "There's one more restriction you should know about. There are often no survivors. Feebies don't work that way."

Eggs twisted the martini glass. "How about I take anything that spills over the edge?"

"Hmmm."

"I won't interfere with Able Team's strategies. I'll just be a protective uncle."

"You got it, but no poaching."

"Thanks, Hal. No poaching."

OUT ON SHELF MASTER NO. 9, Able Team finished their preparations for the terrorists.

"Shit," exclaimed Schwarz, readjusting his earpiece. "They found my little insects."

Pol looked at him. "How do you know?"

"Razul just said, 'Allah's Blade out,' and then they died."

"Do you think they'll change targets?" Pol asked.

"No. These Libyans are a rigid lot. At most they'll change their timing. Let's review our battle plan again."

Unknown to Able Team, the Flying Dutchman they'd missed rested under their feet, waiting. He had hidden on the cellar deck, staying close to a collection of rams and valves called the blowout preventer stack. He had caught enough of Able Team's conversation to know what was coming—a chance to balance the books.

Born in Indonesia, Peeter De Zonderhundt had grown up in Djakarta, on the island of Java. His family, third-generation Dutch traders, had died in a raid by Moluccan communists. The only surviving De Zonderhundt had gone to sea and then to America.

"Go to America," his father had said. "Where anybody, even an Indonesian Dutchman, can be rich."

When Vietnam broke loose, he joined the Army, ending up in the Special Forces. Wounded, then captured, he was tortured by a Russian-coached North Vietnamese interrogation officer. His hatred of communists multiplied following the mutilation he'd endured. After escaping, he was evacuated to a Stateside hospital. The action ended before the massive warrior could return and balance the books. Still nursing the black rage trapped inside him, De Zonderhundt finished college.

"This is it," he told himself. "These bastards are going to answer to me." He rubbed his old FN-FAL affectionately. He always kept the gun in his personal toolbox.

"Come and get it." The Flying Dutchman rode the crest of revenge's wave. The anticipation of releasing more pain than a sane man should carry transformed him into an emotional time bomb.

Night slipped in, dragging an orange sunset behind it. The stirrings of a squall agitated the water. He remembered the indoctrination speech when he'd joined the Special Forces. They had promised the new recruits they would learn to live off the land, to ignore heat and cold, to eat things that would make a goat puke and to ignore pain that would kill the average man. They had been right.

A small boat bumping the platform's hollow leg whispered in the night. The big man slipped the safety off and set his FN-FAL on full auto. Emotions shut down, and professional killer snapped on.

Buzz Condrona's head rose over the cellar deck. One massive hand wrapped around his throat, and another snatched the Uzi out of his right hand. Without ceremony, his body was laid quietly on the deck. As Peeter raised his hand to chop Buzz's windpipe he released his convulsing victim's neck long enough to hear a hoarse "You fucking idiot."

De Zonderhundt, poised to kill Condrona, stopped. "Buzz?"

Coughing as quietly as he could manage, Condrona demanded, "What the fuck are you doin' here?"

"Same thing you are. Balancing the books."

Buzz grabbed the Dutchman's hand. "Me, too—for the guys we left behind."

Two overage warriors believed they could smell cordite.

25

Genghis opened the Cad's trunk and prodded Ironman in the ribs. "Well, my man, you're not round and flat, but my guess is that if those friends of yours are hungry for action you'll make a pretty good shield."

"They'll shoot through me to blow away your ignorant ass."

Genghis rubbed his nose with an index finger. "They didn't the last time."

"Don't press your luck, asshole." It bothered Lyons that Able Team had refused to sacrifice him for the good of the mission. He shrugged, deciding to take care of that little problem when he saw Blancanales.

"Here, cover your ass with these."

Lyons didn't need two invitations. While pulling the pants on and discarding the hospital gown he could see light filtering through the bottom of his bandage. A sense of well-being flooded over him.

Three carloads of killers, preoccupied with the next hour, hustled their gear onto the dock. Ironman, surrounded by three men, followed Alonzo Black. Returning fishermen, tired and late, ignored everything but their watches.

Even with a squall blackening the ocean, the marina's lights kept the area well lit. Ramps reaching out to the boats reflected moisture from the coming storm's damp breath.

War bags and men filled the net tenders within five minutes. Alonzo Black carried his bacteria.

The terrorists roared out of the harbor. Sitting in the dark north of the sea-wall entrance, Eggs watched their departure and rechecked his H&K.

"Easy," he warned his partner. "Don't get aggressive. Our commitment is to patrol the edges. Let 'em run ahead. We've got sniperscopes."

Echoes of the excited voices of the day's sport fishermen rose and fell like a Windsurfer bouncing in the wake of a powerboat. A light fog, typical of California's coast, swirled. A friend to no one, the neutral gray mist cloaked both America's unsung heroes and her dedicated enemies. To further tease the combatants, clear patches of fog-free darkness appeared and vanished.

A RUSSIAN ALFA-CLASS SUBMARINE rolled next to a bouncing pair of rubber boats. Preparing to shove off for Shelf Master No. 9, eight men calmly rechecked their weapons. All were equipped with new laser spotting sights.

"We are close to our hero's medals," the leader in the first boat said to the submarine's skipper.

"Comrade commander, I congratulate you on convincing General Mousa to allow you to back up the Brotherhood."

Comrade Captain Stefan Popov was in a better mood. After a tour in Afghanistan and a teaching stint in the war college, he'd itched for combat, the only measure of a man. Killing and dying were the only significant events in a warrior's life. Being assigned to this mission had been an honor. He saluted the submarine's commander.

"Three hours—pickup." He turned to the other team officer. "Comrade Lieutenant Bespros, we have the health of the motherland in the palms of our hands." The submarine slipped quietly beneath the agitated black water before the teams had rowed thirty feet.

EXCEPT FOR the standard creaks and groans caused by the rising sea, only the sound of No. 9's chugging pump broke the silence. Pol finished his fifth complete patrol of the rig and barge. Sitting on the only illuminated object in the area made him uneasy—like in Nam, when a rookie turned on a flashlight on a riverboat. Responsibility rode heavy on Blancanales's shoulders.

"Bugged AK-47 coming, due east."

"It's about time," Pol stated. "Watch for Carl. They'll use him for a shield, and he'll be yelling for us to fire on through."

Cowboy Kissinger had the sensation of being on a stage just before curtain time. Schwarz and Blancanales had choreographed every possibility with precision. Primary strikes, fallback, cross fire, grenades, automatic fire, high ground loss and secondary ambush, all had been taken into consideration.

KHALID SENT Lieutenant Fessi and two of his men ahead as point. The quality of their training showed. Someone had hammered patience, the mark of the pro, into them. They made a textbook approach, never exposing more than one man at a time, and even he was protected with a cross-fire cover.

Seeing no one, Fessi hand-pumped the second wave into action.

Genghis, with a still-bandaged Lyons, climbed to the deck. He pressed his Desert Eagle against Ironman's throat.

Lyons broke the silence. "Anybody out there? Shoot!"

Instead of trying to control his prisoner, the big Chinese leader slugged Lyons across the head, knocking him down. Ironman lay on the cold steel deck. Color drained from his face.

Seeing his combat partner crumple into a heap almost forced Blancanales to overreact. Almost. It took the blue-steel discipline learned during his years with Able Team to hold him in check.

Allah's Blade hit the deck, followed by Omar Khalid. They spread out.

"Where's Black?" Razul demanded. Pointing with his swagger stick, he shouted, "Tabina! Secure the barge. Get Black.

"Genghis, get your team into the crew's quarters. Remember, no survivors."

Blancanales's stage whisper penetrated the gray fog. "That was our plan."

From the edge of visibility Pol made out the heavily armed terrorists. Only their eyes moved. Their faces looked frozen, as if they had been touched by a sorcerer with a sense of humor. Their breathing halted. Water dripped from their noses. Then, discipline overrode fear of the unknown. Weapons released from fear's grip, they scanned every probable location.

"We planned annihilation, too," Gadgets yelled, adding a frag grenade to his shout. Its rattle on the diamond-plate deck promised death. The deadly sphere skittered across the platform, then bounced over the side in the direction of the barge.

"Tabina!" Colonel Razul raced toward the edge. "Grenade!"

Schwarz's present exploded in midair. Yellow petals streaked through the night seeking victims. Some clattered on the deck, ricocheting, leaving orange sparks behind. One fragment burned through the palm of the maverick microbiologist's right hand. Another grazed Ziyad's daughter across the forehead.

Black screamed. "I'm hit! Help! Somebody help me! I'm going to die!" Dropping the suitcase, the microbiologist gripped his wrist and stared at the pumping blood. His voice softened. Shock reigned. He staggered across the barge and fell, whimpering.

Blood trickled into Tabina's eyes. She brushed it away. Then, to absorb it, she shifted the read headband Genghis had given her. In two strides she made it over to the huddled scientist.

She removed her belt and double-wrapped it around his arm, slipped it through the buckle and cinched it down. "Hold this, or you'll lose more blood." Without looking back, she headed for the stuttering firefight.

The frag served as Able Team's trigger.

Schwarz, standing in the darkness provided by the mud-pumping shed, singled out the point team. With his M-16A-2 on rock-and-roll, he fired at Lieutenant Fessi. Tiny clouds of fabric dust exploded across the Libyan's chest as slugs slammed through his camouflage shirt. Some exited his back. Others tumbled around his chest cavity, destroying his heart and lungs. His brain refused to let his finger pull the trigger.

Fessi's two support men turned and tried to pick off Gadgets. Schwarz caught one with a burst. His head exploded. A misty cloud replaced the corpse's skull. His body twisted and crumpled to the deck.

Two wounded and two dead within seventeen seconds. Razul knew he was in for a battle. He'd made his mark in combat, and now, by Allah, he'd use his warrior skills. He dropped behind the crane long enough to identify the firing positions.

Standing with one foot on each side of Ironman's body, Genghis spotted Blancanales. Luckily, the L.A. hood carried the AK with a beeper in the stock and the firing pin removed. Carefully he centered the sights on Pol's throat and squeezed the trigger.

Nothing.

He pulled the bolt back and let it snap back into place, then zeroed in on Pol's chest and squeezed. Same result.

Genghis slammed the AK down and jerked out his Eagle. Knees bent, holding the Israeli automatic with both hands, he selected the Able Team warrior's chest.

Blancanales's first round hammered through his left bicep. The Chinese hood's Desert Eagle flew off into the darkness.

"The Eagle has landed," Pol yelled, still on target. A second and then a third slug connected with his left thigh. Genghis collapsed on top of his unconscious captive.

Two Horde men remained. Saving their leader was now more important than the mission. Firing randomly at the machinery room and the mud-pumping house, they recovered Genghis, dragging him behind the bulk tanks. They ripped his shirt into strips and applied tourniquets.

Razul, still watching from his position behind the crane, viewed Genghis's fall with mixed emotions. Hatred for the Chinese criminal clouded his regret at the loss of his backup.

Cowboy Kissinger announced his presence with a rebel yell after taking out the third of the dead lieutenant's team with a 3-round burst in the chest. The dead terrorist's last statement from his Kalashnikov hummed through the air over Gadgets's head.

The yell triggered old memories in Omar Khalid. He recalled first hearing a similar sound when he'd been five. Born a prince of a rich tribe, he had never lacked for anything. Great status came automatically with being the favorite son.

Then the Americans had come. He could still visualize his father shaking his head in wonderment at the amazing machines the foreigners had brought to steal their oil.

These barbarians had raced their jeeps up and down the dunes, laughing and slapping each other. Khalid's contempt for them was boundless.

Comrade Major Khalid wanted Cowboy Kissinger. A Texas cowboy was a symbol of America, his hated enemy.

BELOW, ON THE CELLAR DECK, Peeter and Buzz held themselves in check.

"Let 'em get over the first-contact jitters," Buzz suggested.

De Zonderhundt nodded in the dark. "I got a feeling these bastards got some backup somewhere. Let's lie low for a while."

SCHWARZ WAS NERVOUS about the firefight. Ironman lay unconscious in the middle of the killing ground. The hit that Genghis had given Lyons with his ACP had been hard enough to give him a serious concussion. A chill shuddered through Gadgets. He imagined how his partner felt, lying out there on that cold steel deck.

Soon, soon, old buddy, we'll have this firefight over with. Hang in there.

From the darkness of the machinery shack, Gadgets covered most of the deck. He couldn't see the area of the large crane and the helicopter pad, but he did have a clear view of the entrance to the crew quarters.

That was how he spotted her.

She moved with the grace of a jungle cat. Blood dripped from under her red headband and down her right cheek. Tabina made all the right moves. She stayed in the shadows, stopped, checked her position and then moved into the workers' homes.

"Payback time," Gadgets muttered.

While Schwarz slipped behind her, Colonel Razul made his move. He slid under the pipe rack and crawled until he had a view of the area between the mud tanks and the machinery shack. He laid down a barrage of 3-round bursts at the open machinery room door.

One round hit a piece of Gadgets's gear. He spun aside, rolled to his feet and fired his M-16A-2 at the running communist colonel.

Razul disappeared behind the north end of the small shack before Cowboy could pick him up.

Shit, Schwarz complained to no one in particular. My NSA radio has just been trashed. He threw it on the deck before dashing from the shed to the crew quarters.

No lights. He left them out. She might be in a darkened room. He'd be blind to her position in a lit hall. Gadgets wondered if she could see in the dark. She moved like a leopard. Ambush time. Realizing that he'd carved out an impossible task for himself, Schwarz backed down the hall and returned to his original position. He drew fire from the bulk tanks.

From his perch on the helicopter pad, Cowboy's overview confirmed Pol's battle plan. Unless something strange happened, the operation's success looked certain. Then he realized Razul's daughter had disappeared.

He scanned the barge. Alonzo Black still sat on the barge, nursing his hand wound. After the grenade had exploded, Tabina had climbed back up to the working deck.

"Cowboy to Able Team. Tabina missing. Watch your back."

"Gotcha, Pol out."

There was no response from Schwarz.

"Gadgets, state condition."

Only the chugging of the platform's iron holstein pumping money from the oil pool under the Santa Barbara shelf disturbed the night. A confused sea gull landed on the stiff leg of the big crane, squawked, then deserted the warriors.

"Gadgets, state condition. Over." Cowboy tried again.

Pol interrupted. "Cover me. I'm going to check." Blancanales sprinted from his post to the mud tanks and then to the machinery stack. Drawing three bursts on his dash, Pol hit the shed at a dead run.

"Hi there."

"You okay?" Blancanales panted.

"Lost my radio—lucky shot from the good colonel."

"Tabina's gone."

"She's in the crew quarters. I started after her but realized there was no way to avoid an ambush without covering fire."

Just as Pol was about to answer, a tug whistle sang out.

"What the hell was that?" Pol asked Cowboy over the radio.

"Just what it sounded like—a tug. It's docking against the barge."

It didn't make any sense. Why would a tug return to the rig at night? Who had sent it? Blancanales shook his head.

"Give me your radio," Gadgets said. He immediately turned to the international emergency channel.

"Coast Guard, Coast Guard. This is schooner *Albatross*, number A17824BC, disabled in the oil-well area with engine failure. Need call letters of the tugboat *Pussy Cat*. Repeat—need call letters of tugboat *Pussy Cat*."

Almost immediately the Coast Guard operator replied. "What is your position, *Albatross*?" He supplied the requested frequency. "Do you need other assistance?"

"We're anchored. If we can raise the *Pussy Cat* within an hour, everything will be fine. If not, we'll get back to you. Albatross out."

Gadgets punched in the *Pussy Cat*'s frequency and handed the radio to Blancanales.

Gunfire interrupted them.

FJ hornets snapped through the sheet-metal walls. Able Team's soldiers ducked between two DC generators. Cowboy picked up the action and returned fire.

Rosario pressed the On button. "*Pussy Cat*, *Pussy Cat*, this is the Shelf Master. Who the hell sent you? Over."

"Shelf Master, this is *Pussy Cat*. The barge owner ordered us out. Over."

"*Pussy Cat*, we have a critical situation here. Please back off until we notify you. Over."

"Shelf Master, no can do. Shut down pumping. We're going to hook up immediately. Out."

"Shit." Pol switched to Able Team's channel. "Cowboy, what's your situation?"

"They've pulled in their horns. I lost Razul and his daughter. The rest are licking their wounds between the small crane and the sack bulk tanks. It looks like they realize we're a handful. They're laying down just enough firepower to keep our heads down. What about the tug?"

Before Pol could answer, automatic weapons began chattering between the main and cellar decks.

26

Peeter De Zonderhundt thought he'd seen a rubber boat. He was right. Light from the drilling platform had caught the wet sides of a four-man raft. His sighting confirmed, he sunk deeper into the shadows, snapped his fingers to alert Buzz and waited. Battle adrenaline surged through both Nam vets, triggering long-forgotten skills.

Buzz touched the taller man on the shoulder. "Just another bar fight, old buddy."

"Yeah, but these bastards ain't going home. We're going to close the bar."

Condrona chuckled. "Maybe we should be called the eighty-sixers."

Both listened intently for any sound from the black rubber boat. One word penetrated the foggy darkness.

"Comrade."

Uncontainable joy welled up in the Flying Dutchman. "Russians. I've got Russians rowing right up to me." His savored rage poised itself to become revenge.

A rolling wave surged, lifting the invaders' craft up to the level of the cellar deck. With stealth and strength, De Zonderhundt reached out and grasped Captain Popov by the throat. He dangled the warrior the way he would have a trophy on a fishing dock. With rage-tempered slowness, his massive finger shut off, then crushed, the Russian's arteries and esophagus.

Instead of attacking the Dutchman, Captain Stefan Popov attempted to relieve the pressure on his throat. He knew better. There came a time when all professional warriors hesitated and made the wrong decision. Most died from the mistake. Stefan Popov was dying. A perverse happiness glazed his eyes. Stefan Popov couldn't see his executioner. It was better that way.

The remaining three men, stunned by their captain's strange vertical leap, slammed into action when his body splashed into the ocean. Too late. Buzz shot one in the head, and the Dutchman managed to hit the other two. Lower abdominal wounds allowed the Russians to return fire. De Zonderhundt placed two 3-round bursts in their throats. Severed larynxes, shattered tracheas and exploding spines didn't prevent the exiting rounds from tearing holes in the rubber raft. Gurgling bubbles marked the graves of the terrorist team.

Comrade Lieutenant Bespros listened. Concentrated action meant an ambush. The sudden cessation of the automatic weapons fire without a signal from the captain confirmed it. Here was their chance to get it all. With a smile, the new Russian commander whispered for the men to minimize their profile and maintain silence.

ABLE TEAM HUNKERED DOWN when the firefight broke out below.

Pol wondered what the hell was going on down there. He asked Cowboy if he'd seen anything.

"Nothing, just a lot of muzzle flashes."

A backup team. The Feebies must have joined in, thought Pol. I knew they'd jump in.

Still hidden behind the sack bulk tanks, Khalid raised his eyebrows. The smile of a secret victor passed across his face. He turned to the wounded Genghis.

"My backup."

"Fuck you—and your backup," muttered the delirious hood.

While Khalid and the Horde huddled in safety, Colonel Razul worked his way around the outboard side of the machinery house, under the helicopter pad and into the crew quarters. He found Tabina hiding in the dispensary. She'd bandaged her head wound.

"Beloved Tabina. Are you all right?" Razul reached out and pulled his daughter into his arms.

She stiffened. "I don't need comfort, Father. I need dead enemies for Allah's Blade. It's battle time. Judging by the noise below us, I'd guess Comrade Major Khalid's backup is here. We must exploit the confusion."

"Let's take that tugboat," Razul said. "We can pick up Alonzo Black on the way."

"If we do it right, the rest will stay here and blow each other to pieces." Tabina picked up her AK, gave her father the power-to-the-people salute and headed for the door under the helicopter pad.

LIKE A GIANT OCTOPUS on stiff legs, Shelf Master No. 9 stood proud in the night. Deep in Old Nine's guts, Buzz and De Zonderhundt breathed the heady air of blooded warriors. Fog befriended them. They felt invincible.

Condrona never saw the crimson finger of the Dragunov's laser point at his temple. And he didn't see the second dot trace its silent path across the support column and come to rest on his rib cage.

Exhilarated, he reached out and squeezed his partner's arm. And then the far side of his head splattered into Peeter's face. His heart, so recently happy about balancing the books for his buddies, disintegrated from a burst. He collapsed with the peace of a battle won.

Four small target spots moved toward the Flying Dutchman, but they could not get a fix on him.

His FN-FAL on full automatic, he fired while still airborne. Four Russians tried desperately to spot him with their laser sights. The Dutchman's first burst caught one of the terrorists in the throat, decapitating him. His head tumbled into his teammate's lap, distracting the Russian long enough for him to become a stationary target. He caught two rounds in his open mouth as he yelled his buddy's name.

That left two Russian commandos against De Zonderhundt.

The Dutchman landed on his belly in firing position. He screamed and cut the third Russian in half with a burst too long for a professional.

As he jammed a fresh clip into his rifle, Lieutenant Bespros placed a death spot on his chest. He watched small black holes appear in the red patch.

The Flying Dutchman shuddered and shook his head. Death's black spider spun its web over his consciousness. With revenge's sweet energy, he hindered the spider's efforts.

"This is for Russia." The last Soviet's laser registered its contempt for heroes between De Zonderhundt's eyes.

The spider gained. His web muddled the Dutchman's brain.

With a smile, Bespros caressed the trigger.

A 6-round burst broke the night on old No. 9's right. The lieutenant's body was shredded by an H & K. Comrade Lieutenant Bespros's right trigger finger was still willing, but there was no message from his blood-starved brain to instruct it.

Death closed in on the Flying Dutchman. "I did it," he whispered. "I killed Russians." With a happy sigh, he smiled at the busy spider and died.

Forty yards away, Eggs Pelendo set down an HK-33 with a sniperscope. "Just watchin' the edges, just watchin' the edges." He reached for his radio.

27

Blackness reigned again. Consciousness finally crept back, bringing with it a pulsing ache. Its intensity threatened to force a moan from Carl Lyons. He couldn't remember ever having been warm. He tried one finger. It moved. That's a start, he thought. The rest of his right hand moved. Great. Slowly Lyons unraveled his bandage. He risked his right eye. Even though he lay in the middle of a well-lit kill zone, everything was foggy. Should he blame his sight or the Santa Barbara fog? He tried the other eye. More fog. Shit. Still no answer.

Was Able Team's point man going down? Bet me, Ironman thought. Try again. He opened both eyes. A breeze cooperated. Slowly the fog slid off the deck. Everything cleared.

The throbbing stopped. He ignored the cold. Ironman could see. Able Team's leader would fight again. The free world regained one strong warrior.

A memory of a cartoon with two ragged men chained to a wall in a torture chamber flashed in Lyons's mind. Suspended three feet from the stone floor, starving and beaten, the first victim had looked at the second and said, "Now here's my plan."

That's me, Lyons thought, and he chuckled. Head battered in, lying in the middle of a killing ground, putting together my escape plan.

You betcha.

Slowly the Able Team warrior reoriented himself. The racket of automatic fire rattled below. Everything topside quieted. Not good. We should be forcing the action, he griped. He moved his arm as a signal to Able Team. As an added sign, he formed his thumb and index finger into an okay before slipping into a state of semiconsciousness.

Pol caught the sign and breathed a sigh of relief. "Let's get the guy out of the spotlight."

The tugboat *Pussy Cat* approached the barge and backed in. Elsewhere, another group was considering a move. Major Khalid knew the chances for his operation had disappeared with the first shot, but he could salvage almost everything by taking Alonzo Black and his sample.

"We'll make our way around the pipe rack and the crane. Take cover behind the machinery house," Khalid ordered. "From there we need the ladder."

"Bullshit," Genghis said. "You use the ladder. I'm in no condition to climb. We'll use the crane and a pallet. Lower me to the barge deck."

Khalid barely managed to suppress his laughter. "And who is going to operate the crane?"

"I will," one of the Horde's last soldiers offered. "Then I'll climb down."

Genghis's consciousness competed with shock for control. He shook his head. "I want Lyons with us."

"We'll get our fucking heads blown off if we try to get him," the soldier argued.

"I want him."

The remaining gang members looked at each other. Crossing their leader was not an option. "We need cover fire."

Khalid took a position in the middle of the pipe rack, and one of the Horde soldiers set up between the mud tanks and the crew quarters. The bellowing cowboy on the helicopter pad had to be neutralized. Another Muslim had to pin down Pol and Schwarz in the machinery room.

They laid down a blistering covering fire.

One stream invaded the machinery house. Full-jacketed slugs whined and ricocheted off the steel deck and rattled between the big DC generators.

Half dragged, half carried, Genghis made it to the crane. He leaned against the far side of the mast, panting. The tourniquet cut into his arm. His leg throbbed. Only the thought of recapturing Lyons fueled his desire to stay alive. He clung to his dream of revenge the way a hungry tick clings to a hound's ear. The great Genghis Khan lived through worse battles than this, he mused. I'll make it.

Taken with his own set of problems, Comrade Major Khalid hadn't bothered to look at Allah's Blade's battered hostage. A Horde soldier moved out to drag Lyons's semiconscious body over to the crane. When he turned Ironman over, Omar Khalid realized for the first time who it was—the Yankee pig who'd humiliated him in the gym. He added his firepower to the rest.

BLANCANALES REALIZED he couldn't control the firefight. Pinned down. Shit. But he couldn't accept that. "Gadgets," he ground out from his clenched jaws, "we've taken enough of this crap." He clicked the radio on. The same order went to Cowboy. "Cover me."

Running to his right, Rosario burst out of the machinery shack, firing at the last muzzle flash he'd seen.

No return fire. He spun to his left, looking for targets. Nothing.

Fire broke out from Cowboy's position. "Where the hell are they?" Pol asked Kissinger.

"They've got Ironman again."

"Cowboy, where the fuck are they?"

"The barge. They dragged him out during the cover fire." Cowboy felt guilt's cold blade slice through his heart.

SWINGING ON A PALLET didn't rate high on Ironman's list of things to enjoy. Lying beside an armed man sworn to destroy him had even less charm. Even though he'd managed to remove his bandages, Ironman kept his eyes closed whenever he could be observed.

"I may be nicked, but you're still mine," Genghis threatened.

Lyons couldn't let it lie. "Did you get hurt playing with the big boys?" He expected to pay for his bad-mouthing, but Genghis hurt too much.

The dropping pallet jolted Genghis. A soldier pulled him to his feet.

"You assist your leader and I'll help with his prisoner," Khalid offered, ramming his ACP into Ironman's solar plexus.

Instead of intimidating Lyons, it energized him. Controlled rage, a rarity for the Stony Man warrior, pumped him up. He laughed.

Colonel Khalid slammed his 9 mm Browning against Ironman's temple and squeezed the trigger slowly.

Genghis snarled. "Stop. One second after you pull that trigger your head will be missing." The Muslim leader hesitated and glanced back. An AK was pointed at his face. "He's mine," Genghis hissed.

Swallowing another put-down, the terrorist gritted his teeth and ordered Lyons to walk ahead of him.

Again a cold deck pulled the heat from Ironman, but this time it was exhilarating. He walked straight. He had his sight back, and the terrorist next to him was about to give up the AK he was carrying.

Khalid, reveling in his luck at having his hands on the American, decided to get more out of Lyons. With great care he turned him around to shield himself from Able Team. They backed the rest of the way toward the *Pussy Cat*.

The tugboat had dropped a deckhand onto the barge to assist in tying into her towing bridle. He waited to pull in the tug's lines. Razul requested his help in loading Alonzo Black. Colonel Razul's request sounded so natural that the sailor never suspected anything. Taken captive, an ACP resting at the base of his skull, he signaled to the tug to move in. Tabina and her father ordered the boat close enough to board.

"SHIT. They're using Ironman as a shield again." Pol cursed himself for being so conservative. "Gadgets, raise the *Pussy Cat*."

"By the tail or by the—?" Schwarz saw the look on Blancanales's face and decided to save his humor for another time. The skipper answered.

"What's your situation?" Pol asked.

"I'm being boarded by a group of gun-toting Arabs. They have my deckhand."

A voice interrupted. "Colonel Ziyad Razul and his organization, Allah's Blade, now control this asset. If we're harassed, we'll terminate the crew."

"You're dead, Colonel Razul. Dead." Rosario Blancanales clicked the radio off. "This time we control the action. Cowboy, what's the situation?"

"Entire force is at the far end of the barge, waiting to board. If we're going to stop them we'll need a miracle. They still have Ironman between us."

The Able Team warrior remembered Hal Brognola's voice when he'd warned Pol that the President was watching the operation. Ironman could no longer be considered.

"Let's go for it. When you see targets, take them out. Help Ironman if possible. This mission must succeed, with or without Carl." The last part of the order had barely been audible.

IRONMAN RECOGNIZED the moment to force the action. He waited until they hoisted him aboard. A spinning back elbow into a shocked Latino's face shattered the soldier's nose and cheekbones. Lyons caught his AK before it struck the deck. Half a second later, the Kalashnikov's 7.62 mm teeth chewed the terrorist's head off.

Seeing the crazy warrior with an automatic weapon froze Khalid momentarily. He recovered and ran aft, away from Ironman.

Lyons's next burst reduced the Brotherhood's membership to one. Khalid's soldier shuddered in time with the slugs trashing his chest. Death's finger traced its course to his shoulder. An explosion of bones, too violent for his muscles to contain, erupted. His arm fell overboard.

Comrade Omar Khalid ran alone.

Intact, Able Team charged.

Lyons padded past the cabin, heading toward the wheelhouse. He wished he had his Konzak or his Atchison.

Cowboy Kissinger saw Ironman break loose. His guilt was replaced by an emotional charge that catapulted him from the ladder onto the barge. "Ironman's loose, Ironman's loose."

Blancanales inhaled the good news and joined Cowboy at a dead run, barking orders.

"Take the stern. Gadgets, take amidship. I'll take the bow."

Lyons disappeared around the forward cabin as Schwarz started forward. A side window in the wheelhouse opened. An automatic weapon poked its business end down and toward Ironman. Red-and-white sparks sprayed up from the deck, tracing his steps.

"No, you don't," Gadgets yelled. "His flak vest is at the cleaners." He fired from the hip. With a yelp and then a curse, Razul watched his weapon sail off into the darkness.

Blancanales chose the toughest assignment. He had no body count and no verified number of combatants. Charging into a dark room promised ambush.

He charged.

Straight ahead was the galley. Pol flicked the lights on, scanning the room with his M-16A-2. Spilled coffee testified to the suddenness of the terrorists' takeover. One of the crew lay crumpled below the coffee urn, his left hand clutching his shredded chest. He had obviously been surprised in the middle of a coffee break, and the frozen look on his face testified to massive pain. The handle of his broken cup curled around his index finger. Only the thrum of the big GM diesels broke the silence.

Blancanales tried the skipper's cabin, the head, the first mate's cabin and the crew quarters. Empty. He spotted the hatch to the engine room. Whoever hid aft was trapped between him and Kissinger.

Lights from the rig flooded the aft deck. A big hawser lay twisted where it had been dropped. A towing bridle lay unconnected at the stern. Genghis, his man and Omar Khalid moved to the safety of the engine room. Khalid shifted to the space between the engines. When the soldier dragged Genghis to a safe spot, he settled down in front of the fuel filter. Both entrances to the area were covered.

Blancanales pulled the hatch. Khalid hosed the opening with a swarm of 7.62 mm hornets.

"So that's where you're at," Blancanales said. He radioed Cowboy. "Give me some diversion. Then, at the count of five, c'mon in. Khalid's on the lower deck."

Cowboy pulled the aft hatch open, with the same results. Concentrated fire from the Horde filled the opening.

Kissinger reported back. "Hold it, boss, they've covered both access hatches. Do you have any bangers?"

"Nope, only frags. We won't have anybody to talk to if we frag 'em. The steam from the holes we'd blast in the cooling system would boil them alive. I'd rather have one to take home, if possible."

At the bow, Ironman had worked his way around to the port side of the wheelhouse. His bare feet complained at having to climb the cold steel ladder. He jerked the door open.

Colonel Razul stuck the barrel of an AK in the *Pussy Cat*'s skipper's mouth when he saw the Stony Man warrior. "One step closer and I'll spread his brains all over the windows."

"Shit." Lyons slammed the door.

Able Team had Allah's Blade, the remainder of the Horde and the Brotherhood surrounded but couldn't terminate them. Able Team was stymied.

Temporarily.

28

Through his sniperscope, the FBI agent followed Ironman as he moved toward the wheelhouse. The night vision device magnified the sudden bright light when the Able Team warrior jerked the door open, causing a blinding flash in the scope. The door closed. The agent's normal vision returned.

Lyons paced back and forth like a caged animal.

"Patch me through to Stony Man Farm," Pelendo told his partner. "Hal Brognola needs an update."

"What's up?" Brognola sounded frazzled at the other end of the line.

"I'm on the edge—watching your people work."

"Update me."

The FBI agent in charge chuckled. "I've been in some hot situations before, but these boys of yours are in a class by themselves."

"Forget the testimonial. What's happening?" Brognola snapped. "What about Ironman?"

"Sorry. Ironman's loose and wailing."

A deep sigh revealed the depth of Hal's relief. "Talk to me. What's going on?"

"First, a backup team arrived in rubber boats about fifteen minutes after Allah's Blade and the others landed on the Shelf Master."

"That's a load. Able Team handle them?"

"No. A two-man fire team took them on. Real pros. Unfortunately, they only got seven of the eight."

"Terminated?"

"Both teams."

"Hmmm. Russians?"

"I think so. From a sub. I notified the Navy."

"What happened to the eighth man?"

"Let's just call it policing the edges."

"You identified our helpers?"

Pelendo described the Flying Dutchman and Condrona.

"What about the target?"

"Your people have them contained. It's only a matter of time."

"The bacteria?"

"That's a separate question. Alonzo Black disappeared after Allah's Blade boarded. He went aboard with them. Hit in the hand, I think."

"Eggs." The head Fed chafed, impatient. "What about the fucking bacteria?"

"I don't recall seeing any kind of container."

"Did he have the bacteria with him when he boarded?"

Over the radio, Brognola heard someone yell.

"We're under attack," the FBI agent yelled. "Out."

A SECOND PAIR OF RAFTS from the Alfa-class submarine was launched when the first teams failed to report in or return. Their orders were simple. Get the bacteria or die in the attempt. On their run to the *Pussy Cat* they encountered the FBI. Assuming they were perimeter guards, one boat from the suicide squad attacked.

"Return fire," Eggs barked, unlimbering his H&K.

A stream of 9 mm slugs lifted one of his men off his feet and slammed him against the helm. Blood belched through compressed lips onto his white shirt. His eyes glazed before he pitched forward on his knees. "How?" he gurgled in red, surging death. He fell at Eggs's feet.

Pelendo's professionalism took over. He stepped across his fallen partner, firing at the center of the oncoming raft. A frag grenade was lofted toward the FBI boat. It clunked against the bow, sank six inches and exploded. Pieces of fiberglass burst inward, followed by a foot-high stream of cold ocean. Water poured in over the forward decking of the small inboard.

Eggs could have been standing on a firing range at the academy. He calmly swept the center of the oncoming Russians with his own peculiar method of shooting.

After observing the shotgun's killing efficiency, Eggs had developed his own technique. He wanted the death span of a 12-gauge using double-aught but the rapid fire of an SMG. Time after time he'd seen one shotgunner accomplish more than the boys with the automatics. Rate of fire had always been the big problem with shotguns.

Even though Ironman already used the method, Agent Pelendo's new technique solved the problem for him. He called it the Eggs Beater. It's all in the wrist, he chuckled after disintegrating another target. His method proved the theory that simple is better. Instead of aiming at the center of the mass, he slowly rotated his aim in a continuous figure eight around the middle. On each stroke he managed center fire—plus sweep. The effect was similar to plunging an automatic 12-gauge into a side of beef. Hash.

That was what the center of the Soviet strike team resembled. Exploiting the sniperscope, Eggs, his H&K

rocking, chewed the guts out of the elite death squad. Slugs tore through flesh and bone.

Water rose up to Pelendo's knees before he noticed. Hesitating to change magazines, the Fed realized the return fire had stopped. His boat bubbled, shuddered slightly and slid into the dark water. He snagged a life preserver and his magazine pouch.

ALONZO BLACK HID in a tool locker. Shattered bones protruded from the back of his hand. Still in shock, he shivered. "C-c-can't t-trust anyb-body," he stammered. The skinny microbiologist remembered all too well that Genghis was the only one who'd ever stuck up for him. The metal suitcase between his knees contained the only hope he had of not getting killed. If only he could get to the Horde's leader.

CARL LYONS LEANED with his back to the wheelhouse, just below the windows. "This is all I need. A Mexican standoff." Lyons decided to chance a quick war council with Blancanales. He jogged aft.

"Son of a bitch, it's Ironman." Cowboy laughed. "How ya doin', Homes?"

"Where's Pol? Get him on the radio."

Blancanales answered.

"What's your position?" Lyons asked. "We need to coordinate. Razul is holding the skipper of this tub hostage."

"Gadgets and I are in the crew quarters. Join me in the galley. Gadgets can go forward, and Cowboy can handle the stern."

"You got it."

Pol took a good look at Lyons when he entered the galley, trying to decide if Lyons was in good enough shape to take part. Both sides of his head and face were a dark shade of purple. Hammered twice by Genghis's Eagle and battered from the fight in the trunk, the Ironman looked like the top of a blueberry pie.

"How's your vision?"

"No problems. I can see."

"Feel like helping us out on this one?" Blancanales noted the hesitation.

A muffled *whump* followed by the sound of more than one automatic weapon startled both men.

Ironman looked at Blancanales, waiting.

"Check it out, Carl."

Blancanales's radio hissed. "Cowboy to Pol. We've got visitors. Two rafts of trouble. One's in a firefight with a small inboard. Wait. That one's over. They fragged the boat but got wiped out. Great shooting."

"Can you identify? How many?"

"Three. Can't confirm identity. Guessing Russian. The second team is headed for us."

Blancanales shook his head. If they concentrated on the latest combatants they'd take the pressure off his target, but invaders couldn't be ignored. That cold Nam feeling crept over him. Count-your-balls time again. Either way, his back presented a target.

"Cowboy, check aft for more rafts. That's our first priority."

Just inside the hatch, Ironman watched the black rubber boat. For the first time in his career he sensed his own mortality. Like that boatload of killers rowing steadily toward him, Death could be stalking him right now. Dying was a real possibility. Fear didn't enter the equation. Everything seemed brighter. He shook his head. Must be a reaction from being blinded, he rationalized. Yet he knew it was deeper than that. It was the realization that at any moment Carl "Ironman" Lyons could be put on a shelf—permanently. He felt more alive than he had ever thought possible.

A closer look at the boat surprised Gadgets. The original three dwindled. Now he could only see two. Unknown to Schwarz, one dived under the *Pussy Cat* and came up onto the barge.

Gadgets watched the Russian pair who remained in the boat row with slow, even strokes. They stowed their paddles when they were about ten feet from the *Pussy Cat*. Dragunovs ready, they lowered themselves until only the profile of the raft showed.

Blancanales moved to a position on top of the crew quarters. He whispered to Cowboy on the radio. "Have Gadgets take out our friends in the raft. Use the Beretta. The silencer will minimize the muzzle flash."

Not only would the 93-R be invisible, it would be virtually silent. Kissinger had loaded the ammunition to keep the slugs under the speed of sound. Hermann Schwarz had insisted the tiny hiss it made was the word "*tovarich*." It would be poetic justice that the Russians' death messenger would whisper "comrade."

Five feet from the tugboat, the suicide team made their move. The bigger of the two stretched out to grasp a hemp fender. Three 9 mm greetings hit the invader's left side. He didn't change position or acknowledge that he'd been hit. A surge of the raft pulled his fingers loose from the rope he held. His corpse performed a perfect dive into the black waters off Santa Barbara.

It confused the second commando. His Mongolian comrade's dive could have been just a slip from his overreaching. Crouching down again, he waited for his partner to surface.

Suddenly the deck lights came on, exposing Able Team.

"Shit," Ironman muttered. In his short time as a blind man he'd developed a truce with darkness. It was no longer an enemy, and he felt he had an edge on those who had never experienced the blackness.

Tabina, knowing that they were trapped but unaware of the Russian hit team, had turned the working lights on to expose Able Team. A good tactical move for the terrorists, it got everyone's attention.

Only Ironman hid, unexposed by the light. The door of the wheelhouse flew open with a clang. AK high, Colonel Razul stepped out, screaming, "Attack!"

Gadgets, caught between Allah's Blade's commander and the Russian in the raft, smiled. Still centered on the Soviet, Schwarz ignored the threat behind him. Years of combat with Lyons paid off. Gadgets knew instinctively that his friend would eliminate the danger.

"This is for the deckhand," Lyons yelled. Still on an emotional high, Ironman stepped out and brought the muzzle of his weapon in line with Razul's chest. A 3-round burst hit the terrorist leader in the sternum. All three slugs remained within a one-inch circle. What passed for a heart in the killer's chest now qualified for low-grade terrorist ground round. The remaining energy in the bullets was spent shattering the vertebrae supporting his neck. A Libyan rag doll with a frozen sneer tumbled down the ladder to the wheelhouse.

Schwarz's 93-R coughed, and another commando with a blackened face felt Able Team's anger. His trigger finger froze on the Dragunov, which had been aimed at Gadgets's torso. Unknown to Schwarz, Lyons identified another threat in the dark. One of the missing commandos had Gadgets in his sights.

The Russian never got to pull the trigger.

While everyone's attention centered on the raft and Razul, Tabina slipped out of the wheelhouse and joined Genghis in the engine room.

"Where's Alonzo?" she whispered.

"Who the fuck cares?" the wounded Chinese complained. "I'm trying not to bleed to death."

"Without him, this will all have been in vain," she spit. "I'm going to find him." Allah's Blade's last member slipped out of the engine room and into the crew quarters. She covered each room, brandishing her Browning ACP. No Alonzo. He's got to be in some storage place, she thought, and started over, going through every closet, no matter how small.

"TWO LOOSE OUT THERE," Cowboy signaled over his radio. "Watch your backs."

Still not able to get a round off, Cowboy spent his nervous energy in constant movement. He paced from the winch to the port side, to the stern, to the starboard side, back to the winch.

An engine room hatch burst open. Wild-eyed and incoherent, Omar Khalid performed a complete roll and ended up on his feet facing Kissinger. It was obvious to Cowboy that something had snapped in his opponent's mind. Covered by Khalid's AK-47, Cowboy tried to calm the crazed Libyan. "Easy. Easy. We can work this out."

Alerted by the conversation, Blancanales slipped over to cover Kissinger. He didn't see the black-garbed Russian moving across the barge toward the tug. Gadgets clicked his radio switch to alert Cowboy that the Team was aware of his situation.

"Drop your weapon, infidel," Khalid commanded. "I've been sent to avenge those who have had to live under your pagan ways."

Khalid's voice shifted into a little boy's. Tears coursed down his cheeks. He lifted his weapon as though it weighed too much.

"Your father is watching you," Kissinger tried, hoping to divert the psychopathic major's attention. "He's calling for you."

Confused, Khalid turned to the left, toward the Russian commando. His weapon rotated with his body.

The Russian soldier thought of only one thing: self-preservation. He fired. The slugs hit Khalid in the forearms, blasting the rifle and his hands. The major stood staring in disbelief at the red stubs pumping blood over his splintered bones.

He fell to his knees, weeping. "I tried, Father...I tried." The next burst caught him in the head.

Blancanales pivoted, located the muzzle flash and returned fire. An invisible battering ram hit the Soviet in the chest, knocking him through the air. His back skidded on the dam deck of the barge.

"Heads up," Pol yelled.

29

One down, the second Russian thought. Then his comrade flew through the air, dead before he landed. I'm it, the soldier thought. The only one left to complete the mission—to uphold the motherland's honor.

Boris Semenoff loved the Party. Born to a political professor, he'd been indoctrinated from birth. "The Spetsnaz is the only service for me," he'd bragged throughout his teen years. Training for the elite group of professional killer-athletes had become an obsession. When not studying to meet its intellectual requirements, he'd trained. Then had come a blow from which he'd never recovered. The Spetsnaz had rejected him. With no other choice, Semenoff had joined the Moskaya Pekhota—the naval infantry. Eventually his skills had allowed him to transfer to a small frogman group.

Watching his team destroyed one by one, Boris realized that his only chance was to find the bacteria and leave. He sprinted in the darkness to the north edge of the barge. Crawling with his rifle in his arms, he reached the lowest point of the *Pussy Cat*'s railing. A quick leap put him aboard. He slipped forward to the crew's quarters.

TABINA FOUND ALONZO. She reached for the doorhandle of the cubicle where he sat, huddled and in tears. His self-imposed isolation ended with a flash of light.

Hugging the suitcase of bacteria, he begged, "Please don't hurt me." The microbiologist held up his wounded hand like a little boy trying to earn his mother's sympathy. "Please." Sobbing prevented more begging.

Grasping the handle, Tabina jerked the suitcase from between his knees. Realizing his only protection was being taken, Alonzo wrapped his long arms around it.

"No. It's mine—mine."

Tabina jammed her hand into his neck, seeking a pressure point.

The terrified man pulled back and thrust the case at her. "Take it. Go ahead and take it. It won't do you any good anyway. The formula is not complete."

"You're lying." She grasped his neck again.

Curling himself into the prenatal position, the shaking technician clamped his eyes shut and turned toward the bulkhead.

The terrorist squeezed.

Again Alonzo experienced *Shaolin Na*. A burning sensation engulfed his exhausted brain. He whined. Then he surprised himself.

"Go ahead. I'm a dead man anyway. If you don't kill me, someone else will." Alonzo raised his head in time to see a man slip through the opened door and move silently toward them. The butt of the Russian's assault rifle struck Tabina in the back of the neck. She collapsed without a sound.

The Russian laid the edge of his combat knife against Alonzo's throat. He set down his rifle and opened the suitcase.

"Is that the famous bacteria?" He moved the knife just enough to slice through the skin.

"Don't cut— Yes, yes. Take it. Take it. As long as I have it, someone is trying to hurt me."

An awkward smile sloped across the Russian's mouth. With deliberate slowness, Semenoff shifted his blade to Black's right ear—and cut if off. Blood spurted onto the biologist's shoulder. Alonzo Black retrieved the severed flesh.

"Is this all of your famous discovery?" Holding the flask, Semenoff spoke with a thick accent.

Black tried to hold his ear in place. Seeing the blood run down his wrist, he screamed, "There ain't no more!" He exploded to his feet and raced past the startled frogman. Knowing where his only ally hid, the battered technician headed for the engine room's forward hatch.

"Genghis! Help me!"

A burst of Russian bullets shredded Alonzo Black's spine and kidneys. Momentum carried him into the bulkhead full tilt, leaving a painted red streak in his wake.

In a few quiet strides the Soviet killer made it back to the rail. A quick glance spotted Blancanales. Semenoff snapped off three rounds and dived over the railing for the barge, suitcase clutched to his chest.

Death postponed his touch again. Bullets whined past Rosario's head. He dropped to his belly. Keying his hand radio on, he shouted, "The Russian's on the dock with the bacteria. Get him at all costs. Stop him at all costs."

Two, then three M-16A-2s tracked the dodging frogman. Sparks lit the deck on both sides of his feet, but no one hit the fleeing killer. If he made it into the dark water, they might lose the bacteria. He was closing on the edge.

Ironman raised his AK-47 to his shoulder, aiming slightly to the Russian's right. On full auto, he started at the center of a horizontal figure eight, traveled down, around the end, up and back toward the middle. Before he started the second half, Boris Semenoff ran into Freedom's fist.

Never had he experienced such pain. For a split second before he died, the Russian understood what he'd done to others. Semenoff wanted to fall. Each slug added a little more energy to his body, keeping him on his feet. Three M-16A-2s found him. Suspended on four columns of firepower, his dance was prettier to Able Team than anything the Bolshoi Ballet had ever produced. Semenoff's skull disintegrated. The suitcase bounced, then tumbled against a hatch cover.

With a blood-freezing yell, Cowboy leaped over the railing and recovered Alonzo Black's bacteria.

But the celebration was cut short. Hermann Schwarz laid down his weapon as a small ring of cold steel pressed against his neck—the killing end of a Browning ACP. Cold chills—not from the night—shuddered through Gadgets. Tabina's eyes had a strange glaze. "My father's dead." Her lips moved independent of her face. "Go to the engine room."

She knocked three times. "It's me, Tabina. It's okay."

The Horde's last soldier opened the door a crack. His face split into a wide grin. One of the enemy had been captured. He let them in.

"Who is it?" asked a very weak Genghis from where he sat.

"It's Tabina and a hostage."

"Tabina?"

"We're all that's left, Genghis." She burst into tears as she walked over and cradled his sweaty head. "Let's go out in style," she sniffed. "Let's blow this boat and everyone in it to hell."

The Chinese gang leader closed his eyes, then opened them again. "No. We should not sacrifice ourselves."

He pointed at Schwarz. "Knock him out, but don't kill him."

"What's your plan?" Tabina asked as she knocked Gadgets unconscious with her ACP.

"We'll swap him for a ticket out of here," Genghis answered.

No ONE MISSED the Able Team warrior until Pol pulled a position check. No Schwarz. "Cowboy, Gadgets is missing. Check your area." He yelled at Lyons to do the same.

"Clear in the bow and wheelhouse. Skipper's dead and Tabina's missing," reported Lyons.

"Crew quarters empty—except for Alonzo Black's body," called out Pol.

"Stern's clear. The only place left is the engine room," Kissinger radioed.

Ironman joined Pol in the galley. "We've checked everywhere. Only Tabina and Gadgets are missing. Genghis, his soldier and Tabina must have Schwarz in the engine room," Pol said.

THE AFT HATCH to the engine room flew open.

"Don't shoot," the now-conscious Gadgets yelled. "The room's flooded with fuel. You'll blow the whole damn boat up." He stood, hands on his head, ankle-deep in diesel. Vaporized fuel fogged the compartment. The gurgling of an open line added to the threat.

"I want to see Lyons," Genghis demanded.

"He's not here."

"Get him. Now!" Genghis struggled to keep his voice strong.

Blancanales stayed forward to cover the back door. Ironman remained to face the hood. "My, what a lovely purple you are," Genghis heckled.

"What do you want?"

"Out."

"Not a chance."

"I'll blow this damn boat and you with it."

"That's your decision."

While Genghis and Ironman prodded each other, looking for a weakness, Tabina slipped out the deck hatch. Blancanales failed to notice her approach as she moved silently to his blind side.

It wasn't until she was within striking distance that Pol sensed the danger he was in. He immediately dropped to a crouch position, his right hand moving toward the gun Kissinger had insisted he strap to his lower calf. Blancanales brought the pistol parallel to the floor and fired point-blank into Tabina's ankle.

The slug's impact slammed her leg outward, knocking her off her feet. With a scream followed by a growl, she trained her Browning ACP on Pol's head.

Too late.

Bringing his .38 to bear, he fired again.

The first shot shattered her pelvis, and the second tore upward through her stomach and heart. Her blood-spattered body crumpled to the deck.

Blancanales radioed Kissinger. "It's got to be a trap. Genghis is likely going to risk shooting as soon as he has a clear target."

In a single motion, Cowboy leaped, body-blocking Ironman away from the hatch opening. "Ambush!"

Three muffled rounds whistled through the space previously occupied by Lyons. A maniacal laugh reverberated in the engine room. "Close, L.A. pig," Genghis yelled. "Next time." Genghis's soldier had wrapped his shirt around his weapon to minimize the risk of an explosion.

Waves of diesel fuel still gurgled around Schwarz's feet. The odor of fuel filled his nostrils. He felt like a wick in one hell of a big lantern.

Gadgets moved toward the forward hatch. Genghis had the high ground, but he looked as though he were barely holding on to life. He nodded, then jerked his head erect, glaring at Gadgets. The Horde's last soldier backed against the forward bulkhead.

Keying his radio on, Blancanales sent Kissinger to the wheelhouse, hoping to locate a fire-extinguisher system for the engine room. After they'd synchronized their watches, he reminded Cowboy of Ironman's code word—*careful*. It functioned as the trigger word for action. He'd keep his radio on to allow him to hear Ironman.

Gadgets would remember.

Pol asked for Lyons and outlined his rescue plan.

"Go for it," Ironman encouraged.

"Genghis," Lyons called. "Let's talk. Truce?"

"Truce."

Lyons stepped in front of the opening, Tabina's ACP hidden in the back of his belt.

"You're not going to get out of here alive, you know," Lyons opened.

"That's where you're wrong. What's—" Genghis had to stop and gather his strength to continue "—going to happen is..." Deep, gut-wrenching coughs silenced him.

"Hey, man, what Genghis is saying, man, is if you don't give us a ride to the beach, we're going to blow your dude to pieces."

"Careful."

Schwarz dived into the lake of potential death.

30

Schwarz wasn't the only one wet from head to foot.

Also chilled to the bone, Eggs Pelendo swam to the leeward side of the barge, more than ready to get out of the cold ocean. "All I need is for someone to mistake me for a Russian," muttered Pelendo through stiff lips. "It sure as hell is cold out here on the edge."

A third warrior in the firefight shivered, but from the possibility of his imminent death. In shock from his wounds, Genghis shuddered convulsively. And then a strange calm came over him. He closed his eyes momentarily and thought of his past.

Diesel vapors, competing with the air in the engine room for space, choked the Horde leader, forcing him to cough. The effort brought him back to the present.

"Okay, Lyons, I'm ready. Come and get it." Peace painted a big smile on his face.

From his vantage point at the forward hatch Blancanales trained his M-16A-2 on Genghis.

Seated, with his feet dangling off the deck, the leader of the Horde couldn't twist forward easily. Knowing the end had arrived, he tried with his remaining strength to lean out far enough to see Ironman. Pol's slugs struck him first in the right side, turning splintered ribs into knives.

Leaning over, Blancanales shifted his aim to the right, severing Genghis's head from his jerking body. It tumbled through the air.

LYONS TOOK CARE of the last Horde soldier when Gadgets dived into the fuel. The shots had jerked him up against the main fuel filter. When he fell, he exposed holes left in the filter by Ironman's bullets. They sprayed liquid like a large shower head.

Lyons picked up his AK and charged through the opening, just in time to see Genghis's head bobbing just below the surface.

Dripping fuel, Schwarz gave everyone the thumbs-up sign and headed straight for a shower.

"All right!" Cowboy leaned against the amidships railing. "We did it." He held the recovered suitcase aloft.

Neither Blancanales nor Lyons felt like cheering.

Lyons had come face-to-face with his mortality and with the possibility of a life of uselessness. Everything still had a bright aura around it. Knowing that Able Team had performed magnificently filled him with peace.

Seated beside Ironman, Blancanales rubbed his head. "We paid our dues on this one, Carl," Blancanales stated.

"Yeah. And I learned to appreciate sunlight."

"I learned how to play dolphin in diesel fuel," Gadgets said as he rubbed his hair dry. His eyes were red and swollen.

Leaning back against the railing, Kissinger basked in the victory. He didn't see a pair of black hands reach for his right arm. With a whoop, the Texan disappeared over the side.

Kissinger jerked his hideaway out before he hit the water.

"Don't shoot. It's Eggs. Just balancing the books." He grabbed a rail and pulled himself up and out of the water. "Cowboy hassled me back at the hotel, so I thought I'd just say hello." Pelendo stood in a puddle, shaking.

"Welcome aboard." Pol smiled. "Job's done."

"I know. I've been policing the edges."

AFTER HEARING Able Team's report, Hal Brognola lowered his head onto his forearms. Kurtzman's response to the news of Ironman's health was to let out a loud "All right!"

"Well, uh...well, Hal, I think it would be very good for me to—" Lyons cleared his throat, "—recuperate here in Santa Barbara for a while."

Almost out of earshot, Gadgets called out, "We are shocked at the obvious intentions of our friend, our combat buddy, our..."

Lyons turned away from Schwarz. "How about it, Hal?"

I'D BETTER KEEP these curtains closed, thought Ironman. That window-peeking boss of Sherry's might be spying again.

A light knock froze Lyons. He reached for the door.

"Can I come in?" a soft feminine voice asked. "I won't touch the doorknob until you promise not to jerk me into the room."

Lyons pulled the door open slowly, revealing his date a beautiful inch at a time. Sunlight backlit her tumbling hair. She sparkled. Only her laughing eyes showed in her shadowed face.

Again, Carl Lyons thought how wonderful it was to see. "I've missed you. No direction finder...I promise."

She reached for his face. "I have this rain check...."

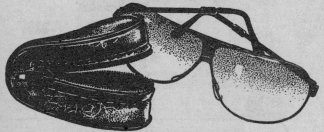

You don't know what NONSTOP HIGH-VOLTAGE ACTION is until you've read your 4 FREE GOLD EAGLE NOVELS

LIMITED-TIME OFFER